RANCHER'S LADY

RANCHER'S LADY

•

Charlene Bowen

AVALON BOOKS
THOMAS BOUREGY AND COMPANY, INC.
401 LAFAYETTE STREET
NEW YORK, NEW YORK 10003

PRINTED IN THE UNITED STATES OF AMERICA
ON ACID-FREE PAPER
BY HADDON CRAFTSMEN, BLOOMSBURG, PENNSYLVANIA

To my longtime friend Eleanor, who can always be counted on to give me that little nudge of encouragement I need.

Chapter One

The stone chapel stood out in stark relief against the cloudy, overcast sky.

As Reese approached the structure, his expression seemed to mirror the dismal weather. A flicker of lightning illuminated his face briefly, accentuating the grim lines of his face and the rigid set of his jaw. He tried—unsuccessfully—to suppress the hollow, empty sensation that gnawed at his insides.

A glance at his watch told him the service would already have started. In fact, it was probably almost over. It wasn't his fault, of course. He'd done the best he could, but there was no way he could have gotten there in time.

It was just as well he was arriving late, anyway, he told himself, so he could slip in unnoticed and not have to talk to anyone. The last thing he felt like doing was listening to people he didn't even know telling him how sorry they were, and having to make the appropriate responses. He just wanted to be left alone to grieve in his own way.

Attending the service—what was left of it—was merely a formality. He couldn't mourn properly in these surroundings, closed in by cold, barren stone walls. Once he was back in Wyoming he'd say his good-byes in his own way, out in the wilderness, with mountains towering in the dis-

1

tance, like sentinels, and the wind blowing fresh and clean. . . .

A sudden clap of thunder jolted him back to the here and now. Squaring his shoulders and drawing a deep breath, as if fortifying himself, he pushed the heavy wooden door open and stepped inside. After taking a moment to allow his eyes to adjust to the shadowy darkness in the rear of the chapel, he located an empty seat in the back row and slipped into it. He tried to concentrate on the service. . . .

"Will you please join me in the Lord's Prayer," the minister was saying.

Amy automatically bowed her head and murmured the words to the familiar prayer. "Our Father, who art in Heaven . . ."

The last few days, as she'd gone through the motions of making funeral arrangements, accepting expressions of sympathy from friends, attending to all the many matters that needed to be taken care of, none of it had seemed real. She'd had the vague feeling she was standing off to one side watching someone else, or that she would soon wake up and find, to her relief, that it had all been a dream.

But it wasn't a dream. She was going to have to accept that her brother Mike and his wife Dina, practically her only living relatives, were actually gone.

It still didn't seem possible. Images played across her mind of the happy, smiling couple, so much in love, at their wedding. She recalled how they'd married after a whirlwind courtship. Dina had come to Seattle from her home in Wyoming to visit a friend from college, and had met and fallen in love with Mike. Instead of returning to Wyoming, she'd stayed here to marry him.

* * *

''Thy kingdom come, Thy will be done . . .''

No! Reese wanted to shout. It *wasn't* God's will. If Dina had stayed in Red Deer where she belonged—where he could look after her and protect her, as he'd always done . . . none of this would have happened.

Although his rational self, the side of him that dealt with logic and common sense, told him how ridiculous that was, he couldn't shake the feeling that somehow he could have—*should* have—prevented her death.

It had been such a senseless accident, Amy thought, one of those things that came out of the blue, with no warning. She'd had vacation time coming, and had offered to come over and stay with Kevin and Chrissie so Mike and Dina could take a trip by themselves, their first since the births of their two children. After a token objection or two, they'd accepted. One minute they'd been on their way to the airport, happily anticipating a second honeymoon. The next, another vehicle, skidding out of control on the rain-wet freeway, had slammed into their car, pushing them into the path of a tractor-trailer. The paramedics who pulled them from the twisted wreckage said they had likely died instantly. . . .

Don't think about that, Amy told herself. In an attempt to shut out the disturbing images, she focused her attention on the various floral arrangements adorning the altar. Before the service started she'd read the cards that came with them. Those roses were from one of Mike's business associates. The arrangement with the gardenias had been sent by a close friend of Dina's. And that large—almost gaudy—arrangement that dwarfed all the others, the one with all the big, showy flowers, was from Stanly Bender. He always did like to make the grand gesture, especially when it suited his purposes.

And in this instance it did, since his purpose was to establish himself as a close family member, and the person most suited to become guardian to his nephew's orphaned children.

He had paid a call on Amy, accompanied by his mousy little wife, Irene, as soon as he'd heard about the accident. "My dear, I can't tell you how sorry I am," he'd said, taking her hand in his. "Now, I don't want you to worry about a thing. I'll handle all the arrangements."

"Thank you, but everything is being taken care of," she'd told him. The last thing she wanted was this unpleasant, overbearing man taking over her right to say her goodbyes to her brother and his wife in her own way.

It couldn't even be said that he meant well. Amy knew him well enough to be sure he was only trying to further his own interests.

"I'll let you know if there's anything I need," she'd said, extricating her hand from his grasp and resisting the urge to wipe off her palm.

If he was the least bit rebuffed by her coolness, he hid it well. "I want you to know Irene and I are prepared to do our duty and open our home to Mike and Dina's poor little children."

Over my dead body, Amy thought, but she'd held her tongue. There was no point in letting Stanly know she'd do anything in her power to keep him from gaining custody of Kevin and Chrissie.

The idea of Stanly Bender having anything to do with the upbringing of her niece and nephew filled her with dismay. If it was true that every family had a black sheep, Stanly certainly fit that role for the O'Brien family. Even her father had acknowledged, despairingly, that his younger half brother had always been something of a problem. Stanly was the kind of person who, in an earlier era, would have been referred to as a ne'er-do-well. Although the quaint, old-fashioned term was seldom used these days, it suited Stanly to a *T*.

There was nothing anyone could really put a finger on. It was just that the man was an opportunist, a schemer who was always looking for a way to further his own interests. And he wasn't above taking advantage of anyone he thought could be of use to him.

Amy and Mike had never cared for him, and after their father's death neither of them had seen any reason to keep up any pretense of a close family relationship with him.

For a while Stanly seemed to have dropped out of sight, and they thought, with relief, that they'd seen the last of their unpleasant relative. He had popped up again, however, like that proverbial bad penny, when Mike and Dina were married. Amy knew it wasn't out of any deep affection for his half brother's children. No doubt he had gotten wind of the fact that Mike had married into wealth. It was no secret that Dina's family was fairly well-off financially.

"... the kingdom, and the power, and the glory forever. Amen," the assembled group murmured in unison.

"The Lord giveth and the Lord taketh away," the minister intoned solemnly. "Into His care we entrust the souls of Mike and Dina."

The finality of those words was like a knife twisting inside Reese, bringing a pain that was sharper, more acute than anything he could have imagined. He had to get out of there. As the organist played a final hymn he stumbled to his feet and, oblivious to the curious glances of those around him, rushed out of the chapel.

Amy realized the service had come to an end.

As the last notes of the organ music died away, she

briefly considered trying to slip out the side door of the chapel in order to avoid having to talk to anyone. By now that little nagging tightness at the base of her skull had erupted into a full-blown headache, and she felt completely drained, both physically and emotionally. She just wanted to go home—although home was, for the time being, Mike and Dina's house.

When she turned around and saw how full the pews behind her were, she quickly abandoned the idea of slipping away. These well-meaning people had also cared about Mike and Dina, and had taken time out of their busy schedules to come and pay their last respects. She was grateful for their support and their sympathy.

As she walked down the aisle toward the exit several people left their seats to fall into step beside her. By the time she was outside she was surrounded by friends and acquaintances, hugging her and offering their condolences.

Her heart sank as she looked up and saw Stanly elbowing his way through the group around her. He reminded her of a shark closing in for the kill.

He frowned disapprovingly as he approached her. "I'm sure you all understand that Amy needs some time to be alone now," he said. "All this has been very difficult for her." With this, he placed a hand on her arm in a proprietary manner and started to draw her off to one side.

At his high-handed manner, Amy's weariness was replaced by a surge of anger. Who did he think he was, dismissing her friends that way? The last thing she needed was Stanly hovering over her, pretending to be concerned for her welfare—especially when that concern was so patently false. She was twenty-seven years old, well past the age of needing a caretaker.

With a brief movement, the kind of gesture one might use to brush away a bothersome fly, she shook Stanly's hand from her arm and took a step or two away from him. It was a deliberate slight, and for a second a little of his aplomb seemed to desert him. The only thing he could do to keep from causing himself further embarrassment was to retreat and stand off to one side. Amy went on talking to those around her as if she'd hardly noticed the brief interruption.

After a while the little group gathered in front of the chapel began to thin out. Glancing around, Amy saw that the minister had engaged Stanly in conversation. While he was thus occupied, she said brief good-byes to those who still remained, thanked them for coming, and made a quick dash for her car.

She breathed a sigh of relief as she drove away. But although she'd managed to evade Stanly for the time being, she knew how persistent he could be. She wouldn't be able to avoid him indefinitely. Sooner or later she was going to have to face him and make it clear to him that there was absolutely no way he was going to gain custody of her niece and nephew.

"Mmm, it smells good in here," Amy said, sniffing appreciatively as she let herself into the entry hall of Mike and Dina's house.

"Aunt Amy's home!" Four-year-old Kevin ran in from the living room and threw himself at her with unbridled enthusiasm. His three-year-old sister, Chrissie, as subdued and quiet as Kevin was outgoing, appeared behind him.

Amy knelt and returned his embrace, also pulling Chrissie into her arms. "What's been going on around here?" As she spoke she gently brushed back the tangle of baby-fine curls that fell across the little girl's forehead.

Unable to stay still for any length of time, Kevin twisted

out of her arms. "Mrs. Howard let us help her make cookies."

"I got to pour the chocolate chips in," Chrissie said in her soft voice.

"I hope you don't mind." Mrs. Howard came in from the kitchen, wiping her hands on a dishtowel. "It gave the little ones something to do. Besides, I thought some comfort food would do you good." The sympathetic, grandmotherly neighbor had volunteered to take care of the children during the funeral, as well as while Amy was out seeing to the many other matters that had to be taken care of after a death in the family.

"That was so thoughtful of you," Amy said, standing up. Kevin ran off into the living room, with Chrissie, always his faithful shadow, trailing behind him. "And thank you for looking after the kids. I can't tell you how much I appreciate all your help."

"It's the least I can do. You certainly have your hands full. Now then, will you need me to take care of them when you go to see the lawyer tomorrow?"

"If it wouldn't be too much trouble. You've done so much already, I feel I'm imposing on you."

"Now, don't you worry about that. Folks have to help each other when something like this happens. Mike and Dina were such a lovely young couple—I couldn't have asked for nicer neighbors. Every time I think of those two babies, left with no parents—" Her voice broke slightly. "I'll be over tomorrow morning so you can keep your appointment," she said, pulling a handkerchief from the pocket of her apron and daubing at her eyes.

Once Mrs. Howard had gone, Amy stood in the middle of the entry hall, her thoughts whirling, wondering, *What do I do now?* For the past few days, ever since the accident, she'd been able to keep from dwelling on the tragedy by focusing on matters that needed her immediate attention—seeing that the proper people were notified, looking after the children, attending to funeral arrangements. Now, however, it was time to start making plans.

Her thoughts were interrupted by the sound of something falling in another part of the house. She almost felt as if she'd been granted a reprieve as she hurried to see what Kevin was up to now. Between thinking up ways to divert Kim and making sure Chrissie received her share of attention, Amy was too busy for the rest of the afternoon to give much thought to other matters.

Fixing dinner for the children, giving them baths, and getting them into their pajamas kept her hands and her mind occupied. Kevin kept up a steady stream of chatter about his friend Dougie from preschool who had a new puppy.

"Could *we* have a puppy, Aunt Amy?" he asked.

"Ah—we'll have to think about that." How could she promise them a puppy? She'd have her hands full enough just looking after two children. And she had no idea where they'd be living or what her job situation would be.

"What's the matter, Aunt Amy?" Chrissie asked as she was being tucked into bed.

Amy summoned a tired smile. "There, is that better? Why don't you say your prayers now."

Obediently, the little girl folded her hands and closed her eyes. When she got to "God bless Mommy and Daddy," a huge lump rose in Amy's throat.

Once Chrissie was snuggled under the covers, she fell asleep almost immediately. Amy paused to take a last look at her before turning the light out. Her glance took in the tangle of curls spread out on the pillow, the high cheekbones, the delicate, babyishly rounded chin. The child looked so much like her mother that Amy had to blink back tears.

It took several demands for drinks of water, and a request that she check under the bed and in the closet to make sure no monsters were lurking about, before Kevin began to yawn and rub his eyes. At last, however, he dropped off to sleep.

All at once the house seemed unnaturally quiet. Amy made a fresh pot of coffee, then puttered around, writing a few thank-yous to those who had sent flowers or notes of sympathy, picking up toys the children had left out, straightening things that didn't need straightening. She was aware that all these tasks were simply busywork.

There was no shortage of more serious matters that needed to be taken care of—decisions to be made that would affect her entire future, as well as the futures of her niece and nephew. She couldn't seem to make her brain function, though. With so many factors to be considered, she barely knew where to begin.

There was no set of doting grandparents on either side to step in and take over. Amy had been in junior high when her mother was struck with the lingering illness that had eventually taken her life. Then, when she was barely out of her teens, her father had died of a heart attack, leaving her alone in the world except for her brother Mike, four years her senior.

Dina, she knew, also had no family to speak of. Her parents had been killed years ago when their private plane crashed, and Dina had been raised by an older brother.

Stanly wasn't even to be considered, of course. She had no illusions about his expressed desire to become guardian to two small children. He'd never been concerned about anyone but himself, and he wasn't likely to change now. The only reason he was exhibiting an interest in taking over their upbringing was to gain control of their inheritance from their mother.

grown up here, and if it was good enough for them it ought to be good enough for Mike's new bride.

Not that she blamed Dina, of course. Dina was such a warm, friendly person, it was hard to believe she could be related to this grim-faced man.

"Don't pay any attention to Reese," Dina had said, when Amy was helping her change from her wedding gown to her traveling clothes after the reception. "He's just a little upset because he always expected me to marry a local rancher and settle down in Red Deer." A dimple twinkled at the corner of her mouth as she added, "He had several prospective husbands picked out for me."

But Amy hadn't found Reese's attitude amusing. "That's positively feudal. Doesn't he realize you're entitled to make your own decisions?"

"You have to understand, Reese has been looking after me ever since our parents died when I was twelve. He was twenty-five then, and I'm sure there were other things he'd rather have done than take on the responsibility of raising a kid sister. He never complained, though. He became— besides my big brother—my father, mother, and best friend, all rolled into one. It's hard for him to let go now, but he'll come around."

Amy supposed he *had* eventually come around. At least, he hadn't disowned Dina. Amy had sensed, though, from remarks Dina had let slip, that he still harbored a bit of resentment over his sister's marriage to Mike, and her decision to live in Seattle.

Her suspicions were confirmed when he didn't show up for the funeral. She'd done everything possible to notify him in ample time. She'd found his phone number in Dina's address book and had tried to call him. After suffering through a series of earsplitting beeps and squawks, she'd been informed by a staticky voice that the phone lines

Because Mike had been adamant about wanting to make it on his own without using any of what he considered his wife's money, Dina had had it put into a trust fund for their children. Although Amy wasn't sure exactly how these matters were handled, she supposed that whatever amount was left after their needs—such as medical and dental care and education—were taken care of, was to be held for them until they were grown. But a clever and greedy guardian—like Stanly—would be able to come up with some creative bookkeeping in order to skim off a substantial amount for himself. The thought of Stanly pretending to care about Kevin and Chrissie only to get his hands on their money made Amy burn with anger.

The only other person who might have any claim on them at all would be Dina's brother, Reese. Amy had met him only once—when he'd managed to tear himself away from his ranch in Wyoming to come to Seattle, ostensibly to attend Dina's wedding to Mike. Amy had suspected he'd actually come to talk his sister out of marrying a penniless nobody and into returning to Wyoming with him.

Even in city clothes, he'd looked out of place, as if he'd be more comfortable out lassoing a steer, or whatever cowboys did. Amy remembered him as being stern and unsmiling, and she'd had the feeling he'd strongly disapproved of his sister's choice of a husband. Even now, she could recall the flash of resentment she'd felt at his obvious conviction that Dina was making a terrible mistake. Who did he think he was, anyway, looking down on Mike as if he weren't good enough to marry a member of the illustrious Cavanaugh family?

And she'd overheard him asking Dina, in an incredulous tone, "You're really planning to *live* here?" What was wrong with Seattle, she'd like to know. She and Mike had were down in that area, due to a storm. She'd intended to give him the opportunity to take part in making plans for the service. After all, it was his right as Dina's brother. After several unsuccessful attempts to reach him, though, she'd finally had to go ahead and make the arrangements herself.

When she hadn't been able to contact him by phone, she'd written him, informing him of his sister's death and letting him know when and where the service was being held. Although she'd rather not have given him that kind of news in a letter, she'd had no choice. It was the only way she could notify him. She hoped mail delivery was more dependable than phone service in that out-of-the-way place where he lived.

But not only had he not shown up for the service, he hadn't even acknowledged her letter. She'd expected that he'd at least contact her for more details of Dina's death, and to ask what arrangements had been made for the care of her children.

Apparently he was still carrying a grudge because he felt Dina had married beneath herself. It was hard to believe he would actually refuse to attend his only sister's funeral because he hadn't approved of her choice of a husband, but he'd obviously washed his hands of her—and of his niece and nephew, the products of that "unsuitable" marriage.

No, she couldn't expect any help from Reese Cavanaugh. Not that she'd want someone like that to have anything to do with Kevin and Chrissie's upbringing anyway.

That left the matter squarely up to her.

A sudden unexpected surge of—admittedly irrational— anger ran through her. Irrational because, of course, there was nowhere she could place the blame, except on the cruel stroke of fate that had left the children orphans—and had put her in the position of being the one to look out for their welfare. It wasn't that she resented having the responsibility thrust on her. She just wasn't sure she was up to it. As much as she loved them, the idea of raising two children on her own scared her half to death.

Her thoughts were interrupted by the ringing of the doorbell. She gave a sigh of impatience. She didn't feel up to hearing any more words of sympathy, no matter how well intentioned they were.

She couldn't pretend she wasn't home, when the lights were on and her car was in the driveway. Arranging her features into what she hoped was the proper expression of welcome, she opened the door.

"Hello . . ."

The word died on her lips as she recognized the man on the doorstep. He seemed even taller than she remembered. Other than that, he didn't appear to have changed much since their single meeting six years ago, at Mike and Dina's wedding. His face was still set into those grim lines.

In all fairness, she had to admit that in this instance that was likely due to grief and loss, rather than disapproval. A twinge of guilt nagged at her as it occurred to her that she might have misjudged him when she'd assumed he simply didn't care, or had washed his hands of Dina. He would be hurting every bit as badly as she was.

She pushed the thought from her mind. If he cared at all about Dina, where had he been for the past several days since the accident? And why hadn't he at least made some attempt to find out if his sister's children were being properly cared for?

"Amy O'Brien? I'm—"

She found her voice. "Reese Cavanaugh," she finished for him. "Won't you come in, Mr. Cavanaugh." She stepped aside so he could enter.

Chapter Two

"Please—call me Reese," he said, stepping inside. He didn't seem to have noticed the coolness in her voice. Or if he had, he chose to ignore it.

"Reese," Amy amended. In the dim light of the entry hall she could see lines of sadness etched on his face. In spite of her feelings of resentment just a few moments earlier, her heart went out to him. He'd also lost someone he cared about very deeply, she reminded herself.

I—I'm sorry about Dina," she murmured. Although the words seemed woefully inadequate, something in his demeanor told her he wouldn't appreciate an overly profuse expression of sympathy. He seemed so . . . untouchable.

"Come have some coffee," she said, opting for a brisk, matter-of-fact manner. "I just made a fresh pot." As she turned and headed for the kitchen she resisted the urge to look over her shoulder to see if he was following her.

She wasn't sure just what her obligation was—there were no guidelines to follow in a situation like this. She felt something was required of her, though. He *was* Dina's brother. "You should have let me know you were coming," she said when they reached the kitchen. ";I could have, ah, made arrangements for a place for you to stay, and had someone pick you up at the airport."

''There wasn't time to notify anyone. I'd been out on the range for several days when your letter came,'' he explained. ''We were having some flooding problems and we had to get the cattle moved to high ground before we lost the whole herd. By the time I got back and found your letter, there was barely time to catch the next flight to Seattle. I got a rental car at the airport as soon as we landed, and headed straight for the funeral.''

For the first time, Amy noticed how tired he looked, as if he hadn't had much sleep in several days. From bits of information she'd gleaned from Dina, she was aware that his spread was fairly large. She'd formed a picture of Reese as a gentleman rancher, who ran the place from the comfort of an air-conditioned office. He'd mentioned being out on the range, though. Now she had the feeling that when he said, ''We had to move the cattle . . .'' he didn't mean he'd stood off to one side giving orders to his crew. Likely, he'd been working alongside them.

''Please sit down,'' she invited, pulling out one of the chairs from around the table. She busied herself at the counter, getting out mugs and spoons, pouring coffee, arranging some of the cookies Mrs. Howard had made on a plate.

Their fingers brushed lightly as he accepted the mug of coffee she held out to him. Although she couldn't say just why, her first impulse was to draw her hand back quickly, as if she'd touched something hot. She had no idea what had caused that sudden, unexpected reaction. Some inner sense told her it was because of a certain air of power and determination that emanated from him. She had a feeling it wasn't something he did purposely, or that he was even aware of; it was simply a part of him.

But that was ridiculous, her common sense said. It was simply that she'd been under a strain the last few days and her defenses were down. Still, when she slid the plate of cookies closer to him, she was careful to keep from touching him.

"Cream? Sugar?" she asked, making an attempt to maintain some degree of composure.

"No, thanks. Black is fine."

She seated herself across from him at the table, then wished she hadn't. Maybe it was because she found his exceptional height intimidating, but she felt she'd have been more in control of the situation if she'd remained standing.

"I wish I'd been able to get word to you in time for you to come to the service," she apologized. "I did the best I could, but—"

"I *was* there," he said. "Just barely. "By the time I arrived it was almost over."

"Oh." She could think of no other reply. She felt a twinge of contrition. Obviously, she'd jumped to the wrong conclusion when she'd assumed he hadn't cared enough about Dina to come to her funeral. "I, ah, didn't see you there."

He picked up a cookie and disposed of it in two bites. "I slipped out as soon as it was over. I didn't feel up to talking to a lot of people."

He said it matter-of-factly, with no apologies. Well, she couldn't fault him for that, she reminded herself, recalling that she'd considered doing the same thing.

"I'm sorry you made the trip all the way here and then missed out on most of the service," she said. "I suppose you'll be heading back soon."

"I'll probably be here for several days," he replied. "Depends on how long it takes to get things settled here."

What "things" would that be? she wondered, with a stab of apprehension. Did he feel he was expected to stay and help her close up Dina and Mike's house and put their affairs in order? If that was the case, she'd make it clear to him—politely, of course—that his assistance wouldn't be needed. She'd managed thus far without his help, and she could handle whatever else came up.

Most likely, though, he simply meant that he'd like to go through Dina's things and take a few items back with him. He'd want some pictures and other keepsakes to remember her by, of course. She'd be glad to help, to point out articles he might like to keep.

For some inexplicable reason, she felt that the sooner he got what he came for and went on his way, the better off she'd be. She couldn't say what it was about him that made her so uncomfortable. He hadn't acted bossy or overbearing. So far, in fact, his manner had been reserved, almost self-effacing. Still, there was something about him that made her quite certain that if they ever faced one another in a battle of wills, he would easily emerge the victor. She sensed that he was a man who was accustomed to getting what he wanted.

He took a long drink of coffee, then set the mug down on the table. "I'll be taking Kevin and Chrissie back to Red Deer with me, of course, as soon as I can make the arrangements to become their guardian."

A multitude of thoughts and emotions tumbled through Amy's mind in rapid succession, beginning with surprise and progressing to anger. Who did he think he was, expecting to just breeze in here and scoop up the kids and whisk them off to some out-of-the-way place?

She realized he was watching her closely, as if gauging her reaction.

"Is there a problem with that?" he asked.

She resisted the urge to snap, *You'd better believe there's a problem!* Forcing herself to display an outward calm, she replied, "It won't be necessary for you to do that. I'm prepared to take over their care."

He raised an eyebrow. "Do you really feel that's a good idea?"

She felt her temper rising. "What right do you have to question my ability to look after them?" she demanded, shushing the little voice that reminded her that just moments before Reese's arrival she herself had been having doubts about her suitability to raise her niece and nephew.

"I'm not questioning your ability," he replied calmly. "I'm just asking you to consider whether you're in a position to take on the care of two young children. I understand your job requires you to travel a lot."

"Yes, I work for an advertising agency, and one of my duties is to call on prospective clients, but—"

"And you live in an apartment."

He'd really done his homework, Amy thought irritably. "What did you do, hire a private detective to check me out and prove how unsuitable I am?"

"Of course not. Dina mentioned, when she was telling me about her sister-in-law, that your job occasionally takes you out of town." He spoke in that infuriatingly patient tone people use when trying to explain something to an unreasonable child. "And I know you live in an apartment because she also said something, in one of her letters, about dropping by there. Has it occurred to you that the kids might be better off with someone who can provide a more, ah, stable home life?"

"You're saying I can't give them a good home just because I travel in my work, and I live in an apartment? My lease is up at the end of this month. I can find a larger place—maybe something with a yard. And I intend to talk to the personnel manager at the agency to see if they have something open that doesn't require traveling."

"And if they don't?"

"There are other jobs," she shot back. "Naturally I'd be willing to look for another kind of work if that was in Kevin and Chrissie's best interests."

He nodded thoughtfully, as if considering this. After a few moments, he asked, "Do you have someone to look after the kids while you work?"

The question sent a flash of anger through her. Did he think she had a sitter or day-care center all lined up, just in case something happened to Mike and Dina and she had to step in and take over the care of their children? "Of course not. I haven't had the chance to look around yet. Do *you?*" she challenged.

"As a matter of fact, yes."

She eyed him suspiciously. What was he trying to pull, anyway? A few moments ago he'd told her he'd rushed here as soon as he'd learned of the accident that had taken Mike and Dina. Yet somewhere along the way he'd apparently found the time to hire a sitter.

Noting her skeptical look, he said, "Mattie Sloan has been keeping house for me for years. She helped me raise Dina after our parents died, and she'd like nothing better than to look after Dina's children. She just turned sixty, and has the energy of a woman half her age."

Mattie Sloan. Amy had often heard Dina extol the virtues of the housekeeper who had obviously been such an important part of her life. "I don't know what I'd have done without Mattie," Dina had said. "When I was a teenager she often had to be the buffer between Reese and me. Reese did the best he could, but he had a tendency to be a little . . . well . . . overprotective. If it hadn't been for Mattie I probably wouldn't have been allowed to date until I was twenty-five."

Although Dina had been exaggerating, of course, Amy

had a sinking feeling at the memory of her words. If Reese had been such a strict, unbending disciplinarian with his own sister that someone else had had to intervene, what kind of guardian would he be for Kevin and Chrissie?

Deep inside, though, she knew she wasn't being entirely fair. Just because he'd been strict with Dina, that didn't necessarily mean he hadn't had her best interests at heart. "I'm afraid I was inclined to be headstrong at times," Dina had admitted with a rueful grin, "and I sometimes rebelled against my brother's rules. It was Mattie who made me understand that the reason Reese laid down so many restrictions was because he loved me and wanted to protect me. She always seemed to know just the right thing to say to get through to me when I was giving Reese a hard time."

The woman sounded like a combination of Mary Poppins and one of those TV mothers from the fifties, Amy thought. She couldn't deny that this paragon of virtue and wisdom would probably do a superb job of raising Dina's children.

She also had to admit that a firm hand such as Reese's might be just what a rambunctious, active little boy like Kevin needed. But what kind of parent would he be for Chrissie? She doubted that he'd understand how shy she was, how easily intimidated. His assertive, take-charge manner would likely frighten her half to death.

Still, though, if it came down to a custody battle, she probably wouldn't stand a chance. It wasn't fair. *She* had expected to become their guardian. Oh, she was aware that it wouldn't be easy. She'd have to do something about her job, find a larger place to live, locate a reliable sitter. None of these problems was insurmountable, though, if she loved Kevin and Chrissie enough. And she did.

She realized Reese was watching her closely. "Look, I don't blame you for feeling resentful," he said, as if reading her thoughts. "I know you were expecting to make a home for the kids, and then I show up, out of nowhere, and try to take them away from you—''

''I have every right to have custody of them,'' Amy interrupted. ''I *am* their aunt.''

''And I'm their uncle.''

He spoke quietly, as if he were simply pointing out an irrefutable fact. Amy could think of nothing to say in return. He was as closely related to Kevin and Chrissie as she was.

And there was no reason to believe he wouldn't make an excellent guardian. There were other factors to be considered, though. He couldn't possibly care about the children as much as she did. He'd never even set eyes on them. Dina had talked about taking them back to Wyoming to meet their uncle and to see where she'd grown up, but had decided to wait until they were a little older before traveling with them. And although she had done her best to get Reese to come to Seattle for a visit, every time she almost had him talked into it, it seemed that some emergency had come up at the ranch that required his immediate attention.

It occurred to her that if he were really as concerned about the kids as he claimed to be, he'd at least want to see them now that he was here.

''You haven't even wanted to know who's taking care of Kevin and Chrissie, or asked to see them,'' she pointed out in an accusing tone, as if that were proof of his lack of any real interest in them.

The lines around his mouth deepened almost imperceptibly, as if he were striving to maintain his patience. ''You mentioned in your letter that you were looking after them. And I didn't think you'd want them awakened at this time of night.''

She could think of no response, since he was right, of course—just as he had been perfectly logical and reasonable in all his arguments. Still, she had no intention of allowing this complete stranger to take away her beloved niece and nephew, just like that. . . .

"We don't have to make any decisions tonight." Reese's voice broke into her thoughts. He rubbed a hand across his eyes wearily. "I'm sure this has been as rough a day for you as it has for me. Besides, it might not be up to us, anyway. Dina and Mike must have left some instructions about who they wanted to be guardian to their children if anything happened to them. Have you talked to their lawyer?"

"Not yet. I have an appointment to see him tomorrow at ten."

"Do you mind if I sit in?"

Actually, she *did* mind, but she couldn't think of any way to come right out and say so without revealing that she considered him her adversary in this matter. She would rather avoid open warfare if possible.

"Of course, you're welcome to be there," she replied.

If he sensed her insincerity, he kept it well hidden. "I'll pick you up around nine-thirty, okay?"

Amy opened her mouth to reply that that wouldn't be necessary, that she would meet him there. She closed it again as she realized he was simply stating his intentions, not asking if it was all right with her. It wasn't worth making an issue over. Something told her she'd be better off conserving her strength for the larger battles she was sure would come.

Getting up, he took one last swallow of coffee. "The kids will be here, won't they?"

She hesitated before answering. Was he just looking for an opportunity to spirit them away? But she was allowing her imagination to run amok. He wasn't going to kidnap them, for Pete's sake. "Yes, they'll be here," she replied.

"A neighbor has been helping me out by looking after them when I have to go someplace. She's coming over tomorrow morning to stay with them."

"Good. I'm looking forward to meeting them." Just before he turned to leave, he paused and looked down at her. "Don't worry too much about this," he said gently. "I know how much those kids mean to you, and I didn't come here with the idea of becoming involved in a tug-of-war over them. After all, we both want the same thing—whatever's best for Kevin and Chrissie. I'm sure something can be worked out."

With that, he turned and went out, leaving Amy peering after him. As he disappeared into the darkness, she had the feeling she'd imagined the whole episode.

A multitude of disquieting thoughts ran through Reese's mind as he drove back to the hotel. The conversation with Amy hadn't gone at all as he'd hoped it would. It had never even occurred to him that she would be so resistant to his plans to take the kids back to Wyoming with him. He'd honestly thought she'd be relieved to have someone else take over the responsibility of raising them.

Lord knew, he didn't want to fight her on this. He knew she had the best of intentions, but surely she must realize she was in no position to provide a proper home for two little kids. Somehow he had to make her listen to reason, to understand that it would be in everyone's best interests for her to give in gracefully and allow him to take over their guardianship. He had a ranch to run, and didn't have time to get involved in a long, drawn-out custody dispute.

He had to admit he could have handled the situation with a little more finesse instead of just barging in like a freight train and announcing that he intended to take the kids away. If he hadn't been so tired . . .

Chapter Three

"Aunt Amy, why can't we go with you?" Kevin asked plaintively, as he and Chrissie watched Amy put the final touches on her makeup.

"I've already explained to you, I have to . . . to take care of some business. Mrs. Howard is coming to stay with you again. Maybe later today we'll go to the park and you can ride the ponies. Would you like that?"

"Yeah, I guess so," the little boy replied, momentarily pacified.

"Good. Now why don't you both go and watch for Mrs. Howard while I finish getting ready." Although Mrs. Howard wasn't due for another ten minutes or so, it would give them something to do.

She frowned thoughtfully as she watched them run off to look out the window. She had intended to tell them Reese was coming over this morning. They'd heard all about their uncle Reese from their mother, of course, and would be excited about meeting him.

She was running late, though, and hadn't had time to break the news to them properly. She'd had trouble getting to sleep last night as she'd replayed, in her mind, the conversation with Reese, and then had overslept this morning. Anyway, she told herself, it was just as well she hadn't mentioned Reese to the kids, on the chance that he didn't show up.

Not that she had any reason to think he wouldn't, of course. Bossy and overbearing though he might be, he had struck her as a man who could be depended on to keep his word. He'd said he'd pick her up at nine-thirty, and very likely he would. She glanced at her watch. It was almost that time now.

Giving her hair a final pat, she stepped back to survey her reflection in the full-length mirror. She looked competent and self-assured. She gave a satisfied nod. That was the impression she'd hoped to convey. She had a feeling she was going to need every iota of confidence she could summon for the coming confrontation with Reese Cavanaugh over custody of Mike and Dina's children. It was important that she make it clear to him she wasn't someone who could easily be taken advantage of. If he thought he could just waltz in and take Kevin and Chrissie without so much as a by-your-leave, he was going to find out he had a fight on his hands.

Still, no matter how determined she was to keep him from gaining custody of the kids, she at least owed him the courtesy of letting them know they were about to meet their uncle for the first time. She'd better get on with it if she expected to do it before Mrs. Howard arrived.

"Kevin, Chrissie," she called, going into the living room. "I need to talk to you."

At her approach the children turned away from the window, where they'd been watching for Mrs. Howard. "Aunt Amy," Kevin said excitedly, "there's a man coming up the sidewalk! A real tall man! He's coming to the door. Should I let him in?"

"No!" Amy cried, more sharply than she'd intended to. "Don't—"

But she was too late. Before she could stop him the boy had the lock undone and was opening the door. "Hi," he greeted the visitor. "My Aunt Amy is home. And me 'n' my sister."

"That's good," Reese said, smiling down at him, "because that's who I came to see—you and your sister." He was carrying a couple of large, irregularly shaped packages.

"Me 'n' my sister . . . ?" Kevin's words trailed off as he studied this tall stranger. "Hey, I know who you are. I've seen lots of pictures of you. You're Uncle Reese, and you live on a ranch in . . ." His brow furrowed in concentration. "In Wyoming!" he finished triumphantly. Pleased with himself, he pulled the door open wider. "Come in," he invited. He turned to look at Amy over his shoulder.

"Kevin, what have I told you about letting strangers in?" she chided, trying to sound stern. After all, she had to make it clear to him that he couldn't go around opening the door to just anyone.

"But Uncle Reese isn't a stranger," the boy pointed out.

Amy opened her mouth to explain to him that he was supposed to find out who was there *before* opening the door. She closed it again, though, as Reese stepped into the entry hall. She had the uncomfortable feeling she had lost control of the situation.

She noticed Kevin eyeing the packages in Reese's arms with interest. She felt a twinge of resentment. Apparently, he hoped to win them over with presents.

"What's in the packages?" Kevin asked with unabashed curiosity.

Amy was going to reprimand him, then decided against it. If Reese thought raising children was going to be a snap, he might as well see, right from the start, that they were real flesh-and-blood kids. They weren't always little models of decorum.

But if Reese felt the boy needed a few lessons in manners, he kept it well hidden. Kneeling down with one knee on the floor, so he was closer to Kevin's eye level, he said, "I brought you something." He looked past the boy to Chrissie, who was standing off to one side gazing at him uncertainly. "I have something for you, too."

Amy watched to see how Chrissie would react. She had a tendency to be shy around people she didn't know. And even though Reese was her uncle, he was still a stranger to her.

Chrissie shot a glance at Amy, as if asking her approval before approaching Reese. When Amy responded with a nod, Chrissie edged closer, peering at Reese over her brother's shoulder.

Reese reached into one of the bags and took out a pair of Western boots with designs etched into the rich, dark leather. He held them out to Kevin. "Here, try these on for size."

"Wow!" Kevin's brief monosyllable spoke volumes. Sitting down on the floor, he started pulling his sneakers off without taking time to undo the laces.

"Now then, sweetheart . . ." He turned his attention to Chrissie, who was still holding back slightly, somewhat in awe of this tall stranger.

His voice had taken on a different, softer tone, and Amy sensed that he was making a special effort not to frighten the little girl.

Reaching into the bag again, he withdrew a second, smaller pair of boots, with delicate cutout designs across the toes and up and down the sides. Chrissie breathed a soft little "Oooh," as she leaned forward to take a closer look. She reached out a tiny hand tentatively, then pulled it back.

"Go ahead, take them," Reese said gently. "They're for you."

Still, she hesitated. Before long, though, her delight overcame her trepidation, and she accepted the gift.

"I hope they fit," Reese said over his shoulder to Amy. "I had to guess at the sizes." Turning back to Chrissie, who was fumbling with the laces of her sneakers, he asked, "Do you want some help?"

After a brief pause, the little girl nodded.

After unlacing and removing her shoes, he carefully worked the boots onto her tiny feet. Amy couldn't help noticing how gentle his movements were, as if he were aware of how easily his exceptionally tall stature could intimidate a small child, especially one already inclined toward shyness.

In a short time both children were proudly stomping around the room, walking with a comical stiff-legged gait so they could admire their new boots, which fit perfectly.

Planting himself squarely in front of Reese, Kevin asked, "What else did you bring us?"

Amy watched Reese closely to see if he was put off by the boy's forthright manner. He seemed unperturbed, however, as he opened the second bag and took out two small Western hats, one in a soft, off-white shade, the other a dark gray.

"Hey, neat!" Kevin exclaimed. "Which one's mine?" When Reese held the gray hat out to him he snatched it up eagerly and plopped it onto his head. "How do I look?"

Giving him an appraising gaze, Reese made a few adjustments. He tilted the hat to one side at a rakish angle, and pulled the brim low over one eye. "There," he said. "Now you look like a cowboy who's all duded up to go into town on Saturday night."

Chrissie had been watching with interest. Now she asked timidly, "Wh-what about me?"

"This one is for you, sweetheart." Reese placed the cream-colored hat on the little girl's head, carefully brushing aside tendrils of fine, silky hair. "Would you like to have a look?"

Chrissie nodded, her eyes wide.

Picking her up, Reese carried her over to the mirror in the entry hall. Her expression lit up in delight when she saw her reflection. After he knelt and put her back down, she regarded him seriously for several seconds. Then, heaving a deep sigh, she twined both arms around his neck in an uninhibited hug.

Amy stared in stunned amazement. Normally, Chrissie was hesitant about even talking to someone she didn't know well. Yet the child had apparently made up her mind—after only a few moments—to accept Reese unconditionally. It was almost as if she knew, intuitively, that this man was someone she could trust and depend on.

An unexpected lump rose in Amy's throat as she watched the tender way he returned the little girl's embrace, as if the child was infinitely precious. When he arose, she noticed that his eyes looked suspiciously moist.

"We'll have to get going if we intend to be at the lawyer's office by ten," he said. Although his tone and manner were brisk and businesslike, she noticed a certain huskiness in his voice. "Didn't you say a neighbor was coming over to stay with the kids? What time is she supposed to be here?"

As if on cue, the doorbell rang. Relieved at the brief diversion, Amy opened the door to admit Mrs. Howard. There was a curious tightness in her throat that would have made it difficult for her to reply right then. She swallowed and took a few deep breaths. By the time Kevin and Chrissie had greeted Mrs. Howard and displayed their new boots and hats to her, Amy was able to perform the proper introductions.

Although Mrs. Howard extended a hand as she acknowledged the introduction, she regarded Reese with a somewhat reproving look. "Mr. Cavanaugh, I'm so glad to see you finally got here," she said, placing a slight but unmistakable emphasis on the *finally*. It wasn't too hard to guess what was going on in her mind. Where had this man been during these last few difficult days when all the funeral arrangements, the care of the children, and the multitude of decisions that had to be made had fallen on Amy's shoulders? her expression seemed to be asking. Why hadn't he been here to do his share?

Instead of attempting to explain why he hadn't gotten there sooner, Reese simply accepted the implied criticism, as if acknowledging he might have been remiss in carrying out his responsibilities. His penitent attitude, along with a boyish smile, was infinitely more effective than anything he could have said in his defense.

"I understand you've been helping out with the children," he said as his hand closed around hers. "I can't tell you how much I appreciate all you've done for Amy—and for Chrissie and Kevin. They're fortunate to have such a kind, unselfish neighbor."

Whether it was due to his complimentary words or the smile that accompanied them, the disapproving look in Mrs. Howard's eyes visibly softened. "I'm so glad I was able to help," she said, looking up at him as if he'd just conferred on her the title of Good Neighbor of the Year.

Amy wasn't sure if she ought to be amused or resentful. What was it about this man that made females, young or old, fall under his spell? It seemed he could charm the socks off them, with no apparent effort.

Well, it wasn't going to work on *her,* she told herself. If he thought he was going to take her niece and nephew away from her just because he could turn on the charm when the need arose, he was in for a disappointment.

Besides, she still wasn't sure she trusted him. Once they were on their way to the lawyer's office, she asked the question that had been on her mind ever since he'd shown up with presents for the kids.

"When did you find time to shop for gifts? I thought you said you barely had time to get to the airport and catch the next flight to Seattle after you got my letter."

As she watched him closely, she noticed the shadow that fell across his features, and the way his jaw tightened. When he replied his voice sounded hoarse, as if he had a catch in his throat.

"I bought those things a few months ago. I'd made up my mind I was going to get out here to see Dina and her kids, if I never got another thing done. I'd already started making arrangements for my foreman to handle things while I was gone. If only I hadn't waited . . ."

As his words trailed off Amy shot a glance at him. He was looking straight ahead, his features revealing nothing of his inner feelings. She sensed that he was hurting. After all, the opportunity to atone for things left undone, for good intentions that had never been carried out, was lost to him forever. Her instinct also told her he wouldn't welcome any expression of sympathy, that he would rather handle his grief in his own way.

They rode the rest of the way in silence, except for Amy's directions to "Turn here," or "Take a left at the next light."

The lawyer, Earl Wingate, faced Amy and Reese across the polished desk. "I'm, ah, afraid we have a bit of a problem."

Reese frowned. "You mean my sister and her husband didn't leave their affairs in order?"

"Well, they did—up to a point."

What the heck does that mean? Reese wondered, wishing the man would get on with it.

"Provisions have been made for the disposition of their community property. It all goes to their children, of course. What there is of it, that is. Mike and Dina didn't have a lot of assets." He cleared his throat. "Even the house is so heavily mortgaged that at this point it's more like a liability."

Reese's jaw tightened. What right did that young pup have marrying Dina if he couldn't even support her properly?

"They were trying to get their computer software business off the ground," Amy put in defensively. "Most of what they made went back into it."

If the lawyer noticed the sudden current of tension between Reese and Amy, he didn't show it. Keeping his tone and manner impassive, he went on. "Dina's legacy from her parents is set up in such a way that it isn't part of their joint estate. It stays in the family and will be held in trust for her children. Of course, funds for their care will be released to whoever is appointed their guardian."

So what was the problem? Reese wondered. He did his best to suppress his impatience, even though he wanted to shout, *Get to the point!*

Earl Wingate shuffled the sheaf of papers on his desk. "It seems that Mike and Dina neglected to specify just who that guardian should be."

"Are you saying there's nothing in their wills about who they want to take care of their kids?" Reese burst out incredulously. "Wasn't it up to you to make sure they'd done that?" There was an accusing note in his voice.

"Ever since their first child was born I've been urging them to name a guardian," Wingate said, ignoring the implication that he'd been remiss in his duties.

"Didn't you impress on them the importance of taking care of this matter?" Reese asked.

The lawyer refused to be intimidated by what Reese obviously considered a serious breach of his professional responsibility. "Mr. Cavanaugh," he said, unperturbed, "I can counsel and advise my clients, but I can't force them into anything. The fact is, they couldn't come to an agreement on who they felt should be appointed guardian."

In all fairness, Reese had to admit he couldn't lay the blame on Wingate. As the man had pointed out, he couldn't force his clients into anything. If someone was at fault, it would be that unrealistic dreamer Dina had married. Dina, of course, would have had the good sense to see that he was the only possible choice to take over her children's upbringing. It would have been her husband who'd refused to listen to reason.

With a brief wave of his hand, Reese indicated that what was done was done—or, in this case, left undone—and there was no point in rehashing the matter. All he could do now was try to rectify the mistakes that had been made.

"I came to Seattle with the intention of taking the kids back to Wyoming with me," he said. "I live on a ranch, and I have a live-in housekeeper who is more than willing to help care for them."

Amy shot him a resentful look. He spoke as if the matter were settled. "The children *know* me," she pointed out. "I'm sure Dina and Mike wouldn't have wanted them to be raised by a stranger—"

"Now just a minute," Reese interrupted. "I'm not a stranger; I'm their uncle, for Pete's sake." He glanced at

Wingate as if expecting the lawyer to confirm that he was the more suitable guardian.

"It's not up to me to make the decision," Wingate said in a pacifying tone. "The court will decide which relative the children should live with."

"Surely the court will see that Kevin and Chrissie will be better off with someone who is familiar to them," Amy said.

"Any judge with a lick of sense would know that a ranch is a better environment for kids than a city apartment," Reese shot back.

Earl Wingate cleared his throat loudly, as if to remind them that bickering back and forth wasn't going to solve anything. "There's one more thing you should know." He glanced over at Amy. "Stanly Bender came in to see me this morning."

"Stanly Bender!" Amy echoed. "What did *he* want?"

"He wanted to let me know he and his wife are prepared to make a home for his 'dear nephew's children,' " the lawyer said dryly.

Reese didn't miss the dismay in Amy's tone, or Wingate's obvious distaste as he spoke of Stanly Bender. He recalled Amy's comment, as they rode up to Wingate's office in the elevator, that Earl Wingate had been her parents' lawyer, as well as their longtime friend. Apparently he was well-enough acquainted with the family to know this person under discussion.

"Who is this Stanly Bender?" he asked.

"He's my father's younger half brother," Amy explained. "My dad's father died when Dad was about ten, and my grandmother eventually married again and had another son—Stanly. Dad never said much against Stanly, but—from little things I've been able to piece together—as a kid he was always in and out of minor scrapes. And some not so minor. As he grew older, he became even more of a problem. He was a teenager by the time Mike and I were born, and when we were kids we always dreaded a visit from Uncle Stanly. . . .'' Her voice trailed off, as if she were recalling some of Stanly's misdeeds.

''I understand he was the apple of his father's eye, and apparently was seldom made to take responsibility for his actions,'' she went on, collecting her thoughts. ''I don't know if that was the reason he turned out the way he did, but the man has never been a lick of good to himself or anyone else.''

''Does this guy, ah, *do* anything?'' Reese asked.

''Oh, he's had a succession of jobs—everything from used-car salesman to investment adviser.'' Her lip curled in distaste. ''I understand *that* little episode almost got him in some trouble. He always manages to stay just ahead of the law, though. He's a troublemaker and an opportunist, and the only reason he has any interest at all in Kevin and Chrissie is because he'd like to gain control of their inheritance.''

Reese shot a look at Wingate. Throughout Amy's denunciation of Stanly Bender the lawyer had been sitting back in his chair, absentmindedly fiddling with a pencil. Now he returned Reese's questioning glance with a barely perceptible nod, as if to indicate that Amy's description had been completely accurate.

''No judge would allow a man like that to—'' Reese began.

''The court certainly wouldn't—'' Amy burst out at the same time.

They both stopped; then Reese nodded for Amy to go on.

''Stanly couldn't possibly be granted custody of the children,'' Amy said. Then her positive tone wavered a bit as she asked uncertainly, ''Could he?''

Wingate rested his elbows on his desk and pressed his fingertips together. ''There is one thing you ought to be aware of. Stanly Bender is a married man. The court will take that into consideration when making the decision. And it could be a deciding factor.''

Chapter Four

Reese was silent as he drove Amy home, mulling over the lawyer's words. He hadn't anticipated any problems when he'd arrived here to take Dina's kids back to Wyoming with him. Amy was the only other person he'd thought might have any claim on them, and he'd expected it would be a simple matter to bring her around to his way of thinking. After all, there was no question that they would be better off with him. What kind of childhood would they have cooped up in a city apartment, being looked after by strangers?

He was sure Amy meant well, but good intentions weren't always enough. A lively, active little boy like Kevin ought to have a man's influence to direct his energy into the proper channels.

And Chrissie . . . The stern lines of his face softened at the thought of the dainty, fragile-appearing child, so like her mother. He felt such a surge of fierce protectiveness it was almost a physical thing.

And now, here was this Stanly Bender, who was only interested in what he could gain for himself, claiming to want custody of the kids. Reese made up his mind he'd do whatever it took to keep the man from having anything to do with them. He realized he was clenching the steering wheel so tightly his knuckles were turning white. Drawing a deep breath, he forced himself to relax his grip.

By the time he pulled into the driveway he'd managed to convince himself that whoever had the responsibility of choosing a suitable guardian for Kevin and Chrissie would rule in his favor. He felt a pang of sympathy for Amy. He honestly didn't want to see her hurt. He'd make it clear to her, of course, that she was welcome to come to the ranch and visit them as often as she liked.

Still, he couldn't suppress a stab of guilt. Those kids meant a lot to her, and he knew how much she was going to miss them. Why did everything have to be so complicated? he wondered. He was just trying to do what he thought was best.

He had intended simply to drop Amy off and head back to his hotel for now. Although he was anxious to get back to the ranch, he couldn't just whisk the kids away as if they were a couple of packages he was picking up at the post office. Although he usually advocated a direct, "let's get down to business," approach in his dealings, in this instance he realized the need to proceed slowly. Despite the fact that his first meeting with Kevin and Chrissie had gone well, who could tell how they might feel about being taken from all that was familiar in their lives? After all, he was still a virtual stranger to them. He couldn't do anything until he had officially been declared their guardian anyway, so he might as well take his time and give them a chance to get to know him.

But apparently he had underestimated the impression he'd already made on them. They were playing in the fenced yard when he pulled into the driveway, both of them wearing their new hats and boots. They rushed up to the gate the second he brought the car to a halt.

"Don't forget, you promised to take us to the park,"

Kevin burst out almost before Amy had her door open. He looked past her to Reese. "You can come too, can't you?"

Reese hesitated. Although the prospect sounded infinitely more appealing than going back to his solitary hotel room, where there was nothing to do but sit around and count the roses on the wallpaper, he felt it wouldn't be fair to Amy. Giving up the kids was going to be difficult enough, and he didn't want to make things worse for her. The least he could do was not to infringe on what little time she had left with them.

"Please," Kevin coaxed. "It's all right with Aunt Amy. Isn't it?" He looked to Amy for confirmation.

"Of course," Amy replied, after a barely perceptible pause. "You're more than welcome to join us." Although her words and manner were cordial enough, Reese sensed she was less than thrilled at the prospect of having him tagging along on their outing. Not that he could blame her.

He glanced at Amy helplessly, holding his hands out, palms up, as if asking, *What do I do now?*

"Ah, Uncle Reese probably has other plans," Amy said, obviously making a last-ditch attempt to extricate both of them from an uncomfortable situation.

"Do you?" Kevin demanded, turning his attention back to Reese.

Reese was about to make some vague excuse about having other matters to attend to, but the words died on his lips as Kevin looked at him expectantly. He heard himself saying, "As a matter of fact, I *don't* have any plans for today."

"Then you *can* come with us, can't you?"

"Please?" Chrissie added her soft voice to her brother's.

With two pairs of eyes looking at him pleadingly, it was difficult to remain firm in his resolve not to intrude on Amy's time with the kids. Casting an apologetic look at her, he said, "Going to the park is exactly what I'd like to do today."

With the air of one who knew when she was beaten, Amy said, "Just give me a minute to let Mrs. Howard know we're going."

When she returned a short while later she had changed into jeans and a loose-fitting sweatshirt with a Seattle Mariners logo on the front. It struck Reese that she looked more like a teenager than someone supposedly mature enough to be responsible for two little kids.

"Hurry up, Aunt Amy," Kevin called impatiently, looking back at Amy. Drawn by the promise of a pony ride, he had grabbed Reese's hand and urged him on ahead. After a moment of hesitation, Chrissie, caught up in her brother's enthusiasm, left Amy's side and ran up to take Reese's other hand.

Reese glanced over his shoulder. "Yeah, Aunt Amy, hurry up," he said with a boyish grin.

He seemed to be having as much fun as the kids, Amy thought. Watching the way Chrissie and Kevin clung to him, she had mixed emotions. Her sense of fairness told her he was entitled to a close relationship with his sister's children. Still, she couldn't suppress a slight resentment that he had so easily won them over. She recalled the time-honored belief that children were good judges of character. She supposed that was in his favor.

On the other hand, though, there was the possibility that he was simply adept at making people like him in order to achieve his own purposes. After all, if he hoped to convince a judge he was the one most suited to become the children's guardian, it would benefit his case if he was on good terms with them.

She hoped he realized that taking on the full-time care

of two young children was more than just fun and games and trips to the park. It was getting up in the middle of the night to comfort them when they were sick or had a bad dream. It was making sure they saw the dentist regularly for checkups and the doctor for inoculations, and seeing that they ate properly and went to bed on time. It was coping with Kevin's occasional stubborn streaks, and finding ways to help Chrissie become more outgoing. She had spent enough time with her niece and nephew to have some idea of all that was involved.

She tried to put her misgivings aside as they rounded a bend in the path and the pony ring came into view.

While Reese bought the tickets, Kevin studied the patient animals. "That's the one I want," he said, pointing to a flashy-looking black with a shiny coat. The lettering etched across the headpiece of the bridle indicated that his name was Midnight.

Reese came back with the tickets just in time to hear Kevin's remark. "How about you, sweetheart?" he asked Chrissie, bending down to talk to her. "Have you picked one out?"

"Umm—that one." Her glance indicated a dappled gray with a placid expression.

Once both children were settled on their respective mounts, Amy and Reese went to stand behind the railing.

Reese had been leaning with his elbows on the wooden bar. Straightening, he looked down at her. "Would you like me to take them for an hour or so, and give you some time to yourself?"

Amy hesitated before answering. There was no doubt the offer was tempting. She couldn't help feeling it would be a cop-out, though, to shift the responsibility to someone else. Besides, a little voice cautioned her, what if he just wanted to demonstrate that he could do a better job of looking after the kids than she could?

"I'm not trying to usurp your authority." Reese's voice broke into her thoughts. "If you'd rather we all stayed together—"

"No," she replied, almost too hastily. She had to stop looking for some hidden motive in everything he said or did. He was offering to give her a bit of a rest, and she'd be foolish to turn him down. Especially since she was desperately weary. "I appreciate your offer," she said. "Just—please be careful to keep an eye on them every minute." She hoped he'd keep in mind that they were just little children.

As Kevin scrambled off Midnight by himself, Reese helped Chrissie down. "Now can we go feed the ducks?" Kevin asked, slipping one hand into Reese's hand and the other into Amy's.

"Tell you what," Reese said. "Why don't we give Aunt Amy a chance to rest while we go and do that."

"That sounds like a good idea," Amy put in. "I am a little tired. I'd like to just sit here on a bench and take it easy for a while. You and Chrissie can go and feed the ducks with Uncle Reese."

A sense of intense relief came over her, as if she'd just had a heavy weight lifted from her shoulders, as she watched the trio head down the path that led to the duck pond. That relief was mingled with the uneasy feeling that this was something *she* should be doing, though. How could she expect to be a proper guardian for the kids if she was so willing to turn them over to someone else?

For the first time, she wavered slightly in her conviction that she was the only person qualified to take care of Kevin and Chrissie. Ever since they'd been orphaned, she'd had this feeling that she'd be derelict in her duty to her brother and his wife if she allowed anyone else to raise their children. Now she had to ask herself if maybe it was her sense of obligation, rather than a sincere feeling that she was the best person for the job, that made her so unwilling to relinquish custody to someone else.

In her own defense, she reminded herself that at the time of the accident she'd been the only possible choice. Stanly Bender wasn't even to be considered, and she'd had no reason to think Reese would have any interest whatever in taking on the care of his niece and nephew. When he'd appeared at her door last night completely out of the blue, catching her off guard, she'd been immediately suspicious of his motives.

Maybe she'd been a little hasty. He did seem genuinely interested in the kids and their welfare. And they had taken to him immediately.

She realized they had been gone quite a while. Just as she was wondering if she ought to go and look for them, they came into view. She hardly dared breathe as she watched their approach.

With the late-afternoon sun shining behind them, she couldn't make out their expressions. Reese was carrying Chrissie, who had her face buried against his shoulder. Kevin was clinging to Reese's free hand. As he walked along, Kevin rubbed the back of his hand across his eyes in a gesture that made him look touchingly vulnerable.

''What do you say we call it a day?'' Reese suggested. ''I think it's about time to head back.''

Chrissie nodded, her face still buried against his shoulder, and even Kevin didn't protest.

Both children were fast asleep before they were halfway home. As they pulled into the driveway Reese glanced over his shoulder and remarked, ''It doesn't look like they're going to navigate under their own steam.'' Getting out of the car, he reached in the back to unfasten Chrissie's seat belt. As he did so, Amy dug out her keys and went to unlock the front door. When she returned Reese lifted the sleeping child from her car seat. ''I'll let you take the light-weight,'' he said. Handing her over to Amy, he reached into the backseat again for Kevin.

''Which room?'' he asked, when they were in the house.

''Down the hall on the right.'' Her arms full, Amy gestured with her chin.

Once she had Chrissie settled down to finish her nap, she peeked into Kevin's room. Reese had removed the little boy's shoes and was pulling a blanket up and carefully tucking it around him. He put a finger to his lips when he spotted Amy, and together they tiptoed out of the room.

''I—I can't tell you how much I appreciate—'' Her voice failed her, and unexpected tears stung her eyelids. She was afraid if she tried to finish what she'd started to say she might burst out crying.

She couldn't imagine why she was suddenly becoming so emotional, but she supposed the strain of the past few days was beginning to take its toll on her. All at once she was inexpressibly tired.

''You don't have to thank me. Those kids are my responsibility too.'' He put a hand on her shoulder. ''It isn't a sign of weakness to let someone else take over some of the load, you know. You don't have to do it all yourself.'' His eyes and his voice were gentle and understanding.

Amy wasn't sure whether it was the kind words or that comforting touch, but she had a sudden urge to rest her head against Reese's chest and sob out all her weariness, all her fears and doubts. She was so tired of being strong, of trying to keep up a brave front. She wanted to draw on his strength, to hear him reassure her that everything was going to be all right.

She could almost feel his arms coming around her to draw her close, could hear him murmuring soothing words of comfort, as if she were no older than Chrissie.

In the narrow confines of the hallway, they were already so close. A slight movement on her part was all it would take. . . .

She was jolted back to sanity by the ringing of the doorbell. As common sense returned she breathed a sigh of relief that she had been brought back to her senses before she made a complete fool of herself. With a feeling of having been pulled back from the edge of a precipice, she hurried to the front door and pulled it open, too flustered to think about looking through the peephole to see who was out there.

"Hello . . ."

Her smile of welcome faded as she found herself face-to-face with Stanly Bender.

Chapter Five

"My dear, I've been trying to get in touch with you all day," Stanly said, reaching out as if to take Amy's hand.

Anticipating his intention, she quickly took a step back, out of his reach. She resisted the urge to snap, *I'm not your dear!* It occurred to her, once again, how much she disliked this man. Everything about him, from his thinning, sandy hair, his washed-out blue eyes, and his pale, freckled skin to his falsely amiable manner grated on her like fingernails screeching down a blackboard.

"I was a little concerned when I couldn't get you on the phone," he said.

"I was out." Amy's reply was clipped. She had no intention of offering this odious man any explanation for her absence. She also had no intention of inviting him in. She stood with her hand on the doorknob, waiting for him to state his business.

"I thought since Kevin and, ah, Cindy will be making their home with Irene and me soon anyway, there's no reason for putting it off," he said. "I'm sure you'll be glad to be relieved of the burden of caring for them." As he spoke, he stepped into the entry hall. Amy had no choice but to step aside.

"I don't consider looking after my brother's children a

47

burden," she replied coldly, not bothering to inform him it was Chrissie, not Cindy. She had a fairly good idea why Stanly was so eager to take the kids home with him. He likely reasoned that a judge would be more inclined to grant custody to him if they were already in his care.

"If you'll just pack what they need for the time being, I can come back later and pick up the rest of their—" Stanly broke off in midsentence as Reese ambled up, looking past Amy quizzically, as if to see who the caller was.

She had to suppress a smile as the two men appraised one another. Reese managed to convey, by the almost protective way he stood just behind her, that he was completely at home here, and Stanly was the interloper.

Undaunted, Stanly stood his ground. Turning his attention back to Amy, he asked, "Do you really feel it's wise for you to be, ah, entertaining a gentleman friend with the children in the house, especially when their parents are barely cold in their graves? We have to think of what's best for them, you know."

Amy's anger blazed at the implication that she was violating some rule of decent behavior. Even if she *had* been—as Stanly so delicately put it—"entertaining a gentleman friend," what right did he have to reprimand her? But before she could deliver the blistering tirade that sprang to her lips, she felt Reese's hand on her shoulder. The light pressure he exerted was a tacit reminder that it wouldn't be a good idea to antagonize Stanly.

She realized he was right. It was easier to maintain the upper hand as long as she could keep Stanly from knowing how strongly she disliked him—and how determined she was to keep him from having anything to do with Kevin and Chrissie. She swallowed her angry words.

Pretending to ignore the implied criticism of her sense of propriety, as well as to her suitability as a guardian, she said, "I don't believe you've met Dina's brother, Reese Cavanaugh. Reese—Stanly Bender." She tossed off the brief introduction in an offhand way, as if to indicate how unimportant she considered Stanly to be.

The play of emotions Stanly was unable to hide—from surprise to consternation—was amusing. This new development could throw a monkey wrench into his plans, his expression said. He recovered his aplomb quickly, though. "Glad to meet you, Cavanaugh," he said, extending a hand. "Sorry you couldn't get here in time for the funeral."

Nothing in Reese's face, except for an almost imperceptible tightening of his jaw, revealed his feelings. "I *was* here for the funeral," he said in clipped tones.

Amy noticed that Stanly winced slightly as Reese's large, powerful, suntanned hand closed over his. When he extricated his hand he looked as if he would like to check it for broken bones, but didn't want to give Reese the satisfaction.

"From, ah, Wyoming, isn't it?" he asked. "I suppose you'll be heading back soon." There was a hopeful note in his voice.

"Not for a while," Reese replied. "There are some matters I need to take care of here."

"Oh?" Stanly prompted.

But if he expected Reese to reveal what those matters might be, he was in for a disappointment. Reese offered no further explanation as to his immediate plans.

After a moment of uncomfortable silence, Stanly returned to the reason for his visit, but he seemed a little less sure of himself. "I'll take the children as soon as you can have them ready."

"That won't be necessary," Amy murmured. "They're just fine here."

"Now, Amy, be reasonable," Stanly said, trying unsuccessfully to hide his impatience. ''Surely you must realize how much better off they'd be with Irene and me.''

That's it! Amy thought. She'd had enough of this sparring. It was time to make it clear to Stanly that there was absolutely no way he was going to have anything to do with Mike and Dina's children. But before she could think of a suitably scathing way of getting this across to him, she was distracted by a noise behind her. Turning, she saw Kevin stumbling sleepily toward her, rubbing his eyes, when he reached her he leaned against her leg.

Now we're making some progress, Stanly's expression seemed to say. Kneeling in front of Kevin, he said, ''Hi there, little fella.'' His tone was artificially hearty.

''I'm not a little fella,'' Kevin muttered sullenly.

''That's right. I forgot what a big boy you are now. How would you and your sister like to come and live with Uncle Stanly?''

Kevin moved even closer to Amy, and wrapped his arm around her leg. He shook his head as he eyed Stanly suspiciously.

For just a moment Stanly's facade of geniality slipped, to be replaced by a frown of annoyance. He recovered quickly, though. ''Sure you would. You'd like it at good old Uncle Stanly's.''

Kevin looked up at Amy. ''I don't hafta go with him, do I?''

''No, honey, of course not,'' Amy reassured him. Automatically, she reached down to brush the hair from his forehead. As her fingers touched his skin, she noticed how warm he felt.

Rising, Stanly glared at her. ''Now listen here—''

''I—I don't feel very good,'' Kevin mumbled, clutching his midsection. ''I think I'm gonna—'' His words were cut off by a choking sound in his throat. He clamped a hand over his mouth.

A look of alarm came over Stanly's face as he recognized what that choking noise meant. He backed away quickly. "Maybe this wouldn't be a good time to take the children home with me," he said. "I'd better wait until the little fellow is feeling better. I—I'll call you soon." With that, he made his exit, tripping over the doorsill in his haste to put as much distance as possible between himself and Kevin.

Amy felt a profound relief as she closed the door behind Stanly. There wasn't time to gloat, however, with a sick child to be tended to. But Reese already had his hands on Kevin's shoulders, ready to rush him into the bathroom if need be. "Are you going to be all right?" he asked.

Kevin drew a deep, shaky breath. "I—I think so," he replied weakly.

Reese glanced at Amy, his expression filled with concern. "Do you think it's something serious?"

Amy recalled how Kevin had coaxed for something from every food vendor's stand they came to, while they were at the park. "It's likely just an upset stomach," she said. "Probably the ice cream was just a bit too much, on top of two hot dogs and a box of popcorn."

Reese looked vastly relieved. Once assured there was nothing seriously wrong with Kevin, he went into action. While Amy settled the child on the sofa, he brought a cool cloth for Kevin's forehead and a glass of ginger ale to settle his stomach. "One of Mattie's favorite remedies for an upset stomach," he said. Although Kevin was still pale and wan, he was clearly enjoying being the center of so much attention.

Reese glanced at his watch. "I hate to go off and leave you with a sick child to look after," he said, running a hand through his hair, ''but I really have to be going. I, ah, have some business I need to take care of.''

Although Amy couldn't help wondering what kind of business he could possibly have in Seattle, she reminded herself it was none of her concern. ''That's all right. I can manage,'' she assured him.

''I didn't mean to imply that you couldn't. After all, you were getting along just fine before I came along. I just meant—well, I thought you might need me to go out and get some medicine or something for Kevin.''

''I don't think that'll be necessary. You go ahead and take care of . . . whatever it is you have to do.''

Reese shifted his weight from one foot to the other, hesitantly. ''I feel like a rat deserting a sinking ship.''

''It's all right,'' Amy repeated. Finally, with a promise to call later to see if she needed anything, he reluctantly took his leave.

Although Amy had insisted that she didn't mind, she felt unaccountably bereft once he was gone, as if her source of strength had been taken from her. She told herself not to be ridiculous. As he himself had pointed out, she'd been managing just fine without him. Still, she couldn't deny that there was something about him—a sort of quiet dependability that made one want to rely on him.

The thought triggered a little warning in the back of her mind. It would be easy to start forgetting that he was the enemy, so to speak, the one who was trying to take the children from her.

By the time Chrissie woke up from her nap, all pink and rosy from sleep, Kevin was almost his usual self. If he was a little more subdued than usual, Amy knew that could likely be attributed as much to the news he had received about his parents as to any physical cause. For the rest of the day he was quiet, and every so often she noticed him staring off into space, his expression thoughtful. *Poor little boy,* she thought. This was a lot for a four-year-old to take in. Chrissie was less a cause for concern. She was little more than a baby, hardly old enough to understand the concept of death.

As the children ate the light supper she prepared—soup, to make up for Kevin's lunchtime excesses—they chattered about the events of the day—meeting their uncle Reese for the first time, the gifts he had brought them, the outing at the park. So far, with the resilience of the very young, they seemed to be accepting the news of their parents' deaths reasonably well. No doubt there would be questions later from both children, and she hoped she would be able to give satisfactory answers.

Once her young charges were tucked in their beds for the night, Amy settled down on the sofa with a basket of clean clothes. Folding laundry would keep her hands occupied, if not her mind. Now, with the house quiet, it was time to start making some of the decisions that could no longer be put off. There were so many plans to be made when—she refused to consider *if*—she was granted custody of Kevin and Chrissie, it made her head swim.

There was the matter of where they were going to live, for instance. Her present apartment, besides being far too small, didn't allow children. Remaining here in the house was out of the question, of course. It didn't belong to her. It was part of Mike and Dina's estate—although, as Earl Wingate had pointed out, it was more a liability than an asset. It would likely have to be sold.

Against her will, memories sprang to her mind of remarks Dina had made about her own growing-up years on the ranch—not only the open spaces and the fresh, clean air, but also the values and discipline she'd learned from doing her share of ranch chores.

Amy pushed the thoughts away. Granted, a ranch probably *would* be a better environment for children than an
apartment in the city, but countless people managed to
grow to normal adulthood without having had that
advantage.

She folded a pair of Kevin's jeans and put them on top
of the stack of clothes, her brisk, efficient movements
seeming to make quick work of any serious thoughts she
might be entertaining that Reese could provide a better
home for the children than she could.

Her methodical mind went on making plans. Once she
found a suitable apartment, the next order of business
would be to hire somebody—she supposed *nanny* would
be the proper term—to look after the children while she
was working, someone kind and understanding, reliable and
trustworthy.

Someone like Reese's housekeeper, Mattie Sloan, a little
voice in the back of her mind prompted, but she deter-
minedly ignored it. Surely it couldn't be too difficult to find
someone here in Seattle who met the requirements. Mrs.
Howard would be ideal, of course, but while the middle-
aged widow was more than happy to lend a hand in an
emergency, Amy knew she wasn't interested in taking on
a full-time job looking after someone else's children. Besides her bowling league and her garden club, she also kept
the books for her son's business.

It occurred to Amy that she had no idea how to conduct
her search. What if she made an error in judgment and hired
someone completely unsuitable? She realized this whole
business of finding just the right sitter was fraught with
uncertainties.

Maybe she ought to consider a day-care center instead,
she thought, but that presented a whole different set of
problems. It would mean shuttling the kids back and forth

every day, and what if her working hours didn't coincide with the hours the day-care center was open? Besides, she'd heard Dina mention that the better centers had waiting lists.

Whatever she decided, the arrangements would have to be made soon, before her vacation time and family emergency leave were over and it was time to return to her job—assuming she still had one to return to. What if she wasn't able to switch to another position at the agency—one where the hours were more regular, and that didn't require traveling?

All at once she felt something close to panic, as it struck her what a monumental task she was undertaking. It wasn't that she was afraid of responsibility. She'd been on her own for a long time. But being in charge of two young lives was an awesome prospect. She had a few acquaintances who were raising children alone, and she'd seen what a struggle they sometimes had trying to juggle work schedules with the demands of parenthood, and never having enough time to do justice to either one.

Her brow furrowed into a frown as she rummaged through the laundry basket in search of a mate to one of Chrissie's dainty, lace-trimmed socks. Would anyone ever solve the mystery of what became of lost socks? she wondered.

But try as she would to concentrate on her search for the missing item, she couldn't shut out that little sense of uneasiness that had been nagging at the edge of her consciousness. She'd been so certain she was the only one qualified to provide a suitable home for Kevin and Chrissie. Now she found herself wondering if she was being entirely fair to them. Reese had the means to care for them properly. He had a ranch, and a wonderful live-in housekeeper.

But there were other factors to be considered, she reminded herself, abandoning the search for Chrissie's sock, and picking up a towel. After all, wasn't she the one who was familiar to Kevin and Chrissie, the one they loved and trusted? So what if they'd taken to Reese immediately? That didn't prove anything. Barney the Dinosaur had had the same effect on them the first time they'd seen him on television.

And what about Reese's feelings toward them? True, he'd been unfailingly patient and gentle with them today, but she reminded herself that spending one day with his niece and nephew didn't necessarily qualify him to be a good parent. Anyone ought to be able to get along with children for that short a time.

The memory of Stanly Bender's brief visit proved the fallacy of that argument, though. Even Kevin had seen through his fawning insincerity.

She knew she was only making excuses, anyway. Some deep-seated instinct told her that Reese's love for the children was real, and that he'd consider no sacrifice too great when it came to their well-being.

As much as it pained her to admit it, there was no denying Reese could give advantages to Kevin and Chrissie that she couldn't. Although the thought of letting them go out of her life left her with a deep, heavy ache inside, she knew the best thing she could do for them would be to step aside and allow Reese to have custody.

There was always the possibility, of course,—although she hated even to consider it—that the court might appoint Stanly the children's guardian. She couldn't imagine why such a decision would be made, but even judges made mistakes.

As she started to fold one of Kevin's T-shirts, she noticed a small tear in the shoulder seam. She placed the garment to one side, making a mental note to put it with some other items that needed mending. With so much to be done, she wasn't sure when she'd get around to doing any sewing. Maybe not until sometime next week.

A sudden lump rose in her throat as it occurred to her that by next week the court might already have made its decision, and the children might no longer be in her care. If the decision was in Reese's favor and he was allowed to take them back to Wyoming, she was sure Mattie Sloan would whip out her needle and thread at the first sign of a tear or a rip. Under her care, Kevin and Chrissie would probably always be properly groomed, hair combed, hands and faces washed, clothes clean, pressed, and mended.

On the other hand, she couldn't picture Stanly's wife Irene seeing to their needs. The insipid little woman barely had the common sense to look after herself, let alone two small children . . .

When the doorbell rang, her first reaction was a sense of relief that she would have some respite from the troubling thoughts running through her mind. That relief was short-lived, though, as it occurred to her that it might be Stanly, making an attempt to regain whatever ground he'd lost this afternoon.

With a frown of irritation marring her forehead, she set the laundry basket aside and went to the door, then caught herself just in time. She reminded herself that even though it was obvious that she was home, she didn't *have* to open the door to Stanly. Maybe if she just ignored him he'd go away.

As she hesitated with her hand on the knob, a low, earnest voice on the other side of the door said, "Amy, are you there? Let me in, please. I have to talk to you."

Surprised, she opened the door to admit Reese. As he stepped inside, his large frame seemed to fill the small entry hall. There was a purposeful determination in his bearing.

Instinctively, she took a step backward, as if she realized

how easily she could be swept away by the sheer force of his personality. Whatever he had on his mind, she hoped he'd get to the point quickly.

He did. "Amy, I think we should get married."

Chapter Six

Amy's jaw dropped in surprise. What kind of trick was Reese trying to pull? she wondered, eyeing him suspiciously.

"To each other?" she blurted out when she finally regained her voice. The words came out in a high-pitched squeak.

"Of course, to each other." He shot her a curious glance, as if she shouldn't even have to ask, when the answer was obvious. Could he have been drinking? The few times she'd seen him he'd been so . . . so levelheaded, but now he wasn't making any sense. She started to edge away from him.

He appeared not to notice. "It would be strictly a business arrangement, of course—a sort of marriage of convenience. We could go and get the license tomorrow morning. There's a three-day waiting period, but that'll give you time to get ready for the trip."

Trip? What trip? The only one going anyplace was Reese. Right out of this house. "I—I think you'd better leave," she said, hoping he'd go without making a fuss. "We can discuss this in the morning."

She reached for the doorknob, but Reese put a hand on her arm, not roughly, but with just enough pressure to detain her so he could make his point. "We can't wait around until tomorrow to start making our plans. If we're going to make this work, there's no time to waste."

She extricated her arm from his grasp. Whatever he was up to, she wasn't going to fall for it.

"I know this is short notice," he went on, "and I'm sorry to spring it on you out of the blue like this. Once you've had time to think about it, though, I'm sure you'll agree it's the perfect solution."

She wished he'd stop talking in riddles. "The perfect solution to what?"

"To keep Bender from getting the kids, of course. What did you *think* I was talking about—" He broke off, as it apparently occurred to him that she hadn't the vaguest idea what he was getting at. "Maybe I'd better start from the beginning."

"Yes," she agreed, "I think you'd better."

"Why don't we go into the other room, where we can talk?" he suggested, taking her arm again. Still too mystified to protest, she allowed him to guide her into the living room.

"After I left here this afternoon I went back to talk to Earl Wingate. That's why I had to rush off in such a hurry. I wanted to catch him before he left for the day. Otherwise I wouldn't have gone off and left you to cope with a sick child—" He broke off. "How *is* Kevin?"

"He's fine. It was just a little stomach upset." Wasn't he ever going to get to the point? "You were saying . . . ? she prompted.

"Ah—where was I?"

"You were on your way to the lawyer's office."

"Oh. Well, I wanted to sound Wingate out, and find out just what it would take to keep Bender from getting the kids," Reese said, picking up the thread of his story. "According to him, the main thing—actually, just about the *only* thing—in Bender's favor is that the courts are more inclined to grant custody to married couples—all other factors being equal. Wingate seems to feel that if either of us was married, that person would be the logical candidate as guardian, since we're both more closely related to the kids than Bender is. That's when I came up with this plan. If we were married to each other, we'd almost automatically be given custody.''

''But we're not . . .'' Amy's voice trailed off as everything began to click into place. ''That's the screwiest idea I've ever heard.''

''Please, just hear me out.''

But Amy had already started to walk away. She had no intention of staying here listening to some crackpot scheme that would never work. He could let himself out.

''You don't want Kevin and Chrissie to be raised by Stanly Bender, do you?''

His words stopped her. She turned around slowly. Hadn't she vowed to do whatever was necessary to keep Stanly from becoming guardian to her niece and nephew?

But Reese's plan was ridiculous, she told herself. ''The reason the court would favor a married couple would be so Kevin and Chrissie could have a stable family life,'' she pointed out. ''I'm sure they wouldn't consider us a 'stable couple' if we got married just to get custody.''

He gave her a look that said, *Give me some credit.* ''Of course, we'd have to make it look believable.''

''You mean, convince people it was a case of love at first sight? Who's going to swallow that?''

''We *have* known each other since Dina and Mike's wedding,'' he reminded her. ''As far as anyone knows, we could have been falling in love all that time.''

''Maybe we could convince some people, but what about

Earl Wingate? You've already talked to him about this, and he'd feel honor-bound to reveal what we're up to.''

There went that look again. ''I had better sense than to let him know what I had in mind. I just sounded him out, in general terms, about what Bender's chances were. He was the one who brought up the point that you or I would be practically a shoo-in if either of us was married.''

He made it all sound so logical. Still, she thought, there was no guarantee his plan would work. ''What if after we went to all that trouble the court still gave custody to Stanly?'' she asked.

''That's a chance we'd have to take. It's not likely to happen, though. I know it's a gamble, but what else have we got?''

Amy considered this for a few moments, before asking, ''Just assuming I did go along with this harebrained idea, and assuming the court did grant us custody, then what?''

''Then you and the kids would go back to Wyoming with me, of course.''

''You expect me to pull up stakes just like that? What about my job? My apartment?''

''You already said you'd change jobs if you had to for the sake of the children,'' he reminded her, ''and that your lease will be up the end of this month. Surely, when something so important as the kids' welfare is at stake, you can put your job- and apartment-hunting on hold for a little while.''

''What exactly do you mean by 'a little while'? How long would we have to carry out this charade?'' Her words held a touch of sarcasm.

Reese ran a hand through his hair. Amy noticed that, for the first time since he'd shown up at her door tonight, he didn't have a ready answer. ''That's something we'd have to play by ear. I guess we'll just have to stay married until we're sure Bender has given up trying to get the kids. Then we can get a quiet divorce or annulment, and you'll be free to come back to Seattle.''

''And Kevin and Chrissie stay with you?''

''Well, of course. That's the whole point.''

All at once Amy felt a surge of resentment. ''So that's how it works. You expect me to go along with your crazy scheme, which is unethical and immoral, not to mention probably illegal, and could likely get both of us thrown in jail—and then when it's over *you* end up with custody of Kevin and Chrissie, but what do I get out of it?''

''What do you want? Money? I can pay you for your help—''

''No, I don't want your money!'' she shot back angrily, sparks flashing in her eyes. ''Do you think you can just buy whatever you want?'' Remembering that the children were sleeping not too far away, she lowered her voice. ''What I want is to be a part of my niece's and nephew's lives.''

''I'm sorry.'' He looked genuinely contrite. ''I didn't mean to sound as if I'm trying to buy you off. Naturally you'll still have a part in their lives. You can come and stay at the ranch as often as you like. You might even decide to remain in Wyoming. You could get a job in Red Deer or one of the other towns nearby. Then you could see the kids regularly.''

''But you'd have custody of them,'' she said flatly.

''Be reasonable, Amy.'' He took a step toward her and raised his hands as if to put them on her shoulders, but dropped them to his sides as she backed away from him. ''We both know the kids would be better off at the ranch, with Mattie to look after them, than cooped up in a city apartment, being cared for by strangers.'' His tone was gentle, not argumentative, as if he were simply pointing out facts that—no matter how painful they might be—couldn't be denied.

Amy opened her mouth to protest, to refute what he was saying, but nothing came to mind.

While she hesitated, Reese went on. "If you really love those kids—and I have no doubt that you do—you'll want what's best for them."

Sudden tears burned Amy's eyelids and a lump rose in her throat. There was no getting around it. Everything Reese said was absolutely true. Hadn't she admitted to herself, just a little while ago, that the best thing she could do for the kids would be to step aside and allow him to have custody?

That didn't make it any easier, though. It would be like giving up a part of herself.

She realized Reese was looking at her expectantly, waiting for an answer. She felt certain he already knew what her decision would be. She had no right to deprive Kevin and Chrissie of the advantages Reese could give them. Still, she couldn't quite bring herself to say the words that would mean she was relinquishing her claim on the two people she loved more than anyone else in the world, the two people who were her only remaining family. . . .

A soft cry from Chrissie's room spared her the necessity of having to reply just then. "I'll go and see if I can settle her down," Amy said. "Usually all she needs is a little comforting." With that, she turned and headed down the hallway.

Reese felt a pang of regret as he watched her leave the room. She looked as if she were on the verge of tears. He wished there were some way he could have avoided hurting her.

Still, he reminded himself, his first obligation was to his sister's kids. He knew, beyond any doubt, that the best place for them was with him. It had nothing to do with Amy's ability, or her dedication to Kevin and Chrissie. It was simply that he was in a better position to give them a good home.

He had to admit he might have handled the situation a little better. She must have thought he was either drunk or crazy when he'd come bursting in like some kind of wild man, insisting she listen to his plan. He didn't blame her for being suspicious of his motives.

He could hear her murmuring little soothing noises, and in a short time Chrissie's whimpers began to subside. He could picture Amy holding the child in her arms, her soft voice and gentle touch comforting the little girl.

In a few moments all was quiet again. Amy stepped out of Chrissie's room, closing the door behind her. She started down the hallway, then stopped to pick up a stuffed toy that had been left on the floor. Straightening, she hesitated and drew a deep breath, as if gathering her strength.

As Reese watched her, it struck him how small and vulnerable she looked. Ever since he'd arrived here—had it actually been just yesterday?—she'd struck him as confident and self-assured, equal to whatever challenge came her way. Now, as she stood in the half-light of the hallway, she seemed to have let down her defenses, at least for a few moments. She looked like someone who had just about reached the end of her resources, and was going on sheer willpower.

Why hadn't he noticed the dark circles under her eyes, or the weary slump of her shoulders? Why hadn't it occurred to him that she'd been carrying a pretty heavy load on those slender shoulders?

All at once he had an urge to put his arms around her gently and draw her close, to comfort her as she'd comforted Chrissie a few moments earlier. . . .

As if she'd suddenly become aware of his sympathy, and was determined to show him she didn't need him feeling sorry for her, she lifted her chin slightly. The barely perceptible gesture seemed to have the same effect as giving herself a mental shake. As he watched, the outward signs of stress and weariness vanished so suddenly that he might almost have imagined them.

"Everything all right?" he asked as she came into the living room.

Amy nodded. "Chrissie was just overtired. She's had a pretty busy day for such a little girl."

Reese wondered if she had misinterpreted his question on purpose. Obviously, she was reluctant to display any trace of what might be construed as weakness. He was relieved that he hadn't acted on that surprising urge he'd had, to take her in his arms and comfort her. The situation was already complicated enough.

She stood across the room from him, still framed in the hallway. "Reese, about that, ah, proposition of yours . . ."

"Yes?" He hoped she was going to tell him she'd decided to go along with it. He was anxious to get the matter settled.

"I'll do it," she said, after a brief pause. "I'll marry you."

Chapter Seven

Amy's spirits sank lower and lower as she looked out the window of the Ford Bronco at the rapidly changing Wyoming landscape. Trees, miniature waterfalls gushing out from between craggy rocks, even a wild animal or two all rushed by in a kaleidoscopic blur.

She glanced over her shoulder at Kevin and Chrissie. She was thankful they were sound asleep, strapped securely into the car seats she and Reese had bought shortly after leaving the airport at Laredo, where the Bronco had been waiting for them. And Reese was silent as he concentrated on steering the Bronco around the numerous twists and turns in the narrow road.

She needed time to sort out her thoughts. Back in Seattle, listening to Reese's logical, persuasive arguments, this had seemed the sensible thing—the *only* thing—to do. With Kevin and Chrissie's welfare at stake, how could she refuse to go along with his plan?

Once she'd agreed to marry Reese, everything had moved so swiftly she'd had little time to ponder the right or wrong of what she was doing. With so many matters to be tended to, the three-day waiting period had sped by. Besides notifying her employer that she was quitting and her landlord that she wasn't renewing her lease, there was packing and sorting to do.

Reese had quietly and efficiently taken care of many of the details of closing her apartment and Mike and Dina's house. After listing the house with a real-estate agent, he had arranged for shipping or storing of the items Amy felt should be saved, and disposal of what was left.

Somehow, during those hectic three days, she'd managed to squeeze in time to shop for something suitable to be married in. Not that it made much difference to her what she wore, since they would be simply going through the motions.

As Reese had pointed out, though, it was important to make it look as if this were a "real" marriage. He was right, of course. Leaving Kevin and Chrissie in his care, she'd made a quick trip to the nearest shopping mall in search of the proper garment to enhance her image as a blissful, dewy-eyed bride. Before long she'd found exactly what she was looking for. Although the white suit was cut in simple lines, the touches of lace that framed the collar kept it from being overly severe.

"It's perfect!" the clerk in the dress shop gushed, when Amy came out of the dressing room to examine her reflection in the three-way mirror. "You'll be a *lovely* bride."

Fortunately, another customer came into the shop just then, so she was spared the necessity of a reply.

When she stopped by Earl Wingate's office to tell him she and Reese were being married, the longtime family friend was so pleased that she couldn't suppress a pang of guilt. "Amy, I can't tell you how happy I am to hear this," he said, giving her a warm hug. "I'm just a little surprised that it all happened so fast. I didn't realize you and Reese were . . . well . . ."

Amy lowered her gaze demurely. She could feel her

cheeks reddening, and she hoped Earl would attribute it to the bloom of being in love. "We, ah, we were attracted to each other when we first met, at Mike and Dina's wedding. Living so far away, though, we just never had the opportunity to, ah, explore our feelings. Then, when Reese came here for the funeral, well, we finally realized we—we were meant to be together." She disliked deceiving this kind-hearted man, but she eased her conscience by reminding herself it was for a good cause.

"Well, that's just wonderful," he said. "I wish you every happiness. I *am* invited to the wedding, I hope."

Amy hesitated. Granted, his presence would lend an air of legitimacy to the proceedings. She had the feeling, though, that if he were there he'd somehow be able to see through their deception. She was about to make some polite excuse about it being just a small, private affair in the judge's office, when she saw that he was looking at her expectantly. She summoned a smile. "We'd love to have you there."

The brief ceremony went off smoothly, except for one uncomfortable moment just after the judge had pronounced them husband and wife. She realized, with a sinking feeling, that he—as well as Earl Wingate and the clerk who had been pressed into service as a second witness—were expecting them to seal their vows with a kiss. And it had to be more than a token peck on the cheek. They had to make it look good.

It was especially important to her that Earl have absolutely no doubt that this was a real marriage, in every sense of the word. If he were called on to attest to her and Reese's ability to provide a stable, loving home for Kevin and Chrissie, she wanted him to be able to do so with a clear conscience.

She'd known, of course, when she'd agreed to this scheme, that there would be times when they would have to play the happy, loving couple for the benefit of others. Surely she could manage this for Kevin and Chrissie's sake. Swallowing to ease the dryness in her throat, she went into Reese's waiting arms.

As she did so she caught his expression, which seemed to be saying, *We might as well get this over with.* She felt a brief stab of resentment. He didn't have to act as though kissing her was a distasteful chore—something to be gotten through.

She told herself to stop being foolish. Hadn't she, just seconds ago, been apprehensive at the prospect of kissing him? She reminded herself they were only playing a part.

But when he pulled her close, the effect of his nearness was so unexpected she had to stifle a gasp. The feeling of being held against that lean, muscular body, the tangy aroma of his aftershave, the overwhelming maleness that emanated from him, all combined into a sudden, overpowering assault on her senses. Her heart slammed against her ribs, and every cell and nerve ending in her body seemed to leap to sudden, vibrant life.

She wondered if Reese was having the same feelings. She was sure he must be when he pulled back just enough to be able to look down into her eyes. His expression was a mixture of surprise and—was it wariness?—as he searched her face.

All at once every instinct she possessed told her to back away, to put as much distance as possible between herself and Reese. Somehow, though, she couldn't seem to make her limbs obey her will. Besides, she reminded herself, people were watching. A feeling of inevitability stole over her as she simply waited for what was to happen next.

His kiss, when it came, was characteristic of the way he

did everything—competent, skillful, and thorough, as if he had accepted the fact that this was something that had to be done, so he might as well give it his best shot.

It was also extremely satisfying.

Had she been able to think clearly, she might have been shocked at her reaction, but she was only aware of an intoxicating warmth that permeated every fiber of her being. At that moment she could have stayed there in Reese's embrace, with his lips caressing hers, forever.

Sanity returned suddenly, as she became aware of amused chuckles coming from those around them. The judge cleared his throat loudly, as if to remind them they had plenty of time for that sort of thing later. The clerk breathed an envious "Wow!" under her breath.

With what little presence of mind she still possessed, Amy twisted out of Reese's arms and took a few steps backward, gathering the fragments of her composure around her like a protective garment.

Somehow she got through the congratulations and good wishes of those in attendance. She supposed she must have made the appropriate responses. By the time she and Reese left the small office, she felt as if her facial muscles were frozen into a perpetual smile.

Once they were back in the car on their way home, Reese glanced over at her once or twice, as if he had something on his mind. She shot him a look that dared him to make any reference to what had happened back there in the judge's chambers. By now she'd told herself that her unexpected reaction had simply been the result of being overtired and under a lot of stress. It didn't mean a thing.

It might have been easier to convince herself, though, if her lips hadn't still been tingling from his kiss.

* * *

Once she and Reese were husband and wife the custody hearing went through without a hitch, and in a surprisingly short time they were appointed Kevin and Chrissie's guardians. As soon as the formalities were taken care of, they were on their way to Wyoming.

Now, on this last leg of the trip, Amy finally had a breathing spell, a little while in which to reflect on what she'd done.

And all at once she was scared to death!

She glanced over at this man—this stranger—who was now her husband. Here she was, married to a man she barely knew, on her way to someplace out in the wilds of heaven knew where. And what about Mattie, and Reese's friends? Would they welcome her, or would they make her feel like an outsider? Had she made a terrible mistake?

As if he sensed her misgivings, Reese looked over and gave her an encouraging smile.

Lord, he thought, she looked as if she were about to face a firing squad. He couldn't blame her for being nervous. He'd come along and practically steamrolled her into agreeing to this marriage. If there had been any other way . . . But marrying her had been the only solution he could think of to keep Bender from getting custody of the kids.

He had an uneasy feeling, though, that this whole affair wasn't going to be as easy to carry off as he'd first thought. What he hadn't counted on was that sudden, unexpected *something* that had sprung up between them back there in the judge's office after their wedding. Hadn't he assured Amy their marriage would be strictly a business proposition? It hadn't escaped his notice, of course, that she was extremely attractive, but he'd expected to be able to exercise some self-control. He was a grown man, for Pete's sake, not some teenage kid.

Once she was in his arms, though, she'd felt so good

there, small and warm and womanly. And her lips, soft and faintly pink, had looked so thoroughly kissable that he'd allowed his mouth to linger on hers for longer than he should have.

At the time he could have sworn she'd been as affected by that kiss as he was. Now he was beginning to wonder if he'd imagined her response. Since then she'd given no indication whatever that anything out of the ordinary had taken place.

Which was just as well, he reminded himself. There was no sense in inviting trouble. When he'd first concocted this idea he should have taken time to consider the problems that could arise from having to carry on the charade around others. He supposed it would have occurred to him if he hadn't been so caught up in his grief over Dina's death and his concern over the children's welfare.

Anyway, it was too late to start having regrets. He'd never been one for looking back on what was over and done with, and wondering if he'd made the right decision.

"Are we almost there?" Amy's voice broke into his thoughts.

"It won't be long now. Just a few more miles." Once he had maneuvered the Bronco around a particularly sharp curve in the muddy road, he turned to look at her. She was leaning her head back and her eyes were closed, her dark lashes a stark contrast to her almost transparently pale skin. He felt a rush of sympathy for her. If these past few weeks had been hard on him, they'd been even more difficult for her.

"Mattie's expecting us, of course. I'm sure she'll have a hot meal ready and bedrooms made up for you and the kids," he said. She certainly looked as if she could use a meal and a good long rest. She could probably do with a little pampering too. He knew he could count on Mattie to see that she got it. The housekeeper loved mothering people, and she would take this fragile-appearing young woman straight to her heart.

His thoughts went back to the phone call he'd made to Mattie, explaining the situation and letting her know when they'd be arriving. It hadn't been a very satisfactory exchange. Here in this secluded valley in Wyoming, telephone service left a lot to be desired under the best of conditions, and anytime there was the slightest hint of a storm in the air it was almost impossible to carry on a coherent conversation. This had been one of those times.

During the first few static-free minutes he'd managed to let Mattie know he'd be home Friday evening, and that he was bringing the kids. The reception had begun breaking up just as he'd started to tell her about Amy. Mattie had kept saying, "What's that? I can't hear you."

"I said I'm married."

"You're worried? What's wrong?" she'd asked, immediately alarmed. "Are the children all right?"

"Not worried." He raised his voice. "The kids are fine. I'm *married*."

A loud crackling on the line drowned out most of her reply. All he could make out was "Who . . . when . . . ?"

"To Amy O'Brien. You know—Dina's sister-in-law." He was almost shouting to make himself heard. "We'll be home Friday evening."

Between bursts of static, he could hear, "About time you . . ."

Whatever Mattie thought it was "about time" he'd done was cut off by a series of ear-piercing beeps and squawks.

He'd been in the process of explaining the situation when a particularly loud crackle of static almost deafened him. Finally he'd given up in frustration. He'd gotten the basics of his marriage of convenience across to her. He could fill her in on the details when he got there.

Which would be very soon. "Almost there," he said to Amy.

At his words, her eyes flew open and she sat up straight, her hands automatically going to her hair to smooth it into place. Her expression was a mixture of relief, curiosity, and apprehension.

He tried to think of something reassuring to say, but his attention was diverted as they rounded the final bend in the road, and the rambling, two-story ranch house came into view. He pulled the Bronco into the driveway and eased it to a stop, a concerned frown creasing his forehead.

Something wasn't right here.

The wide front windows should have been illuminated by a warm, welcoming gleam of light. Instead, complete darkness surrounded the rustic wood-and-stone structure. It looked empty—deserted.

He'd expected Mattie to be watching for their arrival, to come running out the door the second they drove up, savory cooking aromas wafting after her. He wondered if she could be sick, or had met with an accident.

He had no idea what he might find in the house. "Why don't you wait here while I go in and turn on some lights," he suggested to Amy, keeping his voice as casual as possible.

She took a quick look at Kevin and Chrissie, who were still sleeping soundly. "I'll come with you," she said. "I need to stretch my legs. I've been sitting so long I'm stiff."

He wished he could keep her from accompanying him, but he couldn't come up with any way to do so without alarming her. She was already getting out of the Bronco.

He tried to keep his uneasiness from showing as he ushered her in the front door. The second he entered the house he could sense some kind of tension, almost as if there were some kind of . . . *presence* there It was making the hairs on the back of his neck stand on end.

What in the world was going on here? he wondered, fumbling along the wall for the light switch. His fingers found it, and at once the room was flooded with light.

Amy's exclamation of dismay blended with his own.

Chapter Eight

" "S urprise!"

As the exuberant cries died away, Amy breathed a fervent prayer that this was all a dream from which she would soon awaken.

But the balloons hanging from the ceiling, and the crepe paper–bedecked table on which sat a punch bowl and a tiered cake, topped with a miniature bride and groom, were very real. So were the half dozen or so people gathered around the table, beaming happily. A streamer on the wall behind them proclaimed *Congratulations, Amy and Reese*.

She heard Reese's low, muttered, "What the—"

This couldn't be happening, she thought. Reese was supposed to have made sure Mattie understood the circumstances of their marriage. How could he have neglected to do that? When she shot him a reproachful look, though, she could tell by the baffled frown that furrowed his brow that he was as stunned as she was by this turn of events.

Leaning close to him, she said under her breath, "I thought you filled Mattie in on the details."

"I thought I did too," he whispered back.

The phrase "What we have here is a failure to communicate . . ." popped into her mind. She couldn't remember where she'd heard it, but it definitely summed up the situation.

If she'd heeded Reese's suggestion that she wait in the Bronco while he turned the lights on she would have been spared the embarrassment of walking into this with no warning. Reese could have sized up the situation and come back out and explained that these people—she supposed they were his housekeeper, Mattie, and some of his neighbors and friends—were giving them a surprise party. She would at least have had time to arrange her features into the proper expression of pleased astonishment, instead of standing here gaping. She'd sensed his uneasiness, though, and had wanted to see what they were getting into before bringing the kids in.

Anyway, it was too late now to start thinking about what she *should* have done. She felt Reese's hand on her arm, the slight pressure of his fingers a subtle reminder that they were the center of attention. "Just play along," he whispered. "We'll straighten things out later."

She barely had time to summon a weak smile before the group of well-wishers descended on them, all talking and laughing at once. She was able to catch a few phrases as she was passed from one person to another: "So glad to hear Reese finally . . ." "Sure took everyone by surprise . . ." "Hope you'll be happy here . . ."

Once the initial flurry of greetings began to die down, she found herself face-to-face with a tall, angular woman with plain, sensible features. This, of course, would be Mattie. The housekeeper held her at arm's length for a second or two and looked her up and down before giving an approving nod. "I'm glad you're here," she said. "You're just what Reese needs."

Before Amy had time to puzzle over this cryptic remark, she was engulfed in a warm, exuberant hug. Releasing her,

Mattie took a few steps back and said, "We realize it's late, and you're probably worn out from your trip, but we couldn't let you arrive at your new home without some kind of welcome. You probably didn't have time for all the usual wedding festivities before you left Seattle, and—well, every new bride is entitled to have a little fuss made over her."

Amy found her voice. "Th-thank you," she replied, touched by the efforts of these well-intentioned people. She was surprised at the sudden catch in her throat.

"Now then," Mattie went on briskly, "where are those precious children?" Her almost homely face was transformed when she spoke of Kevin and Chrissie.

"They're asleep out in the Bronco," Amy said. "I got them into their pajamas before we left the airport, so they can be put right to bed."

"Mattie can't wait to get her hands on them kids," one of the guests, a stocky, balding, older man, spoke up. "She's been in such a tizzy getting things ready for them, you'd have thought the queen of England was coming."

Mattie seemed to take the good-natured teasing in stride. "I suppose I can wait until morning to start spoiling them. We'd better get them into bed."

"Good idea," Reese spoke up, almost too hastily. "I'll go bring them in right now." He started toward the door.

Oh no, Amy thought. This whole embarrassing mess was his fault. She wasn't going to let him duck out of here that easily, and leave her to face all these people. "I'll help," she said quickly, politely declining all offers of assistance. "They might be frightened if they wake up to unfamiliar faces," she explained.

While Chrissie and Kevin were gently lifted from their car seats and carried upstairs, some of the guests started bringing the luggage in. Mattie bustled about, overseeing the operation, murmuring soft little endearments as she helped settle the children in their beds. Amy noticed how tenderly she tucked the blankets around them, and the wistful note in her voice as she studied the sleeping Chrissie and whispered, ''She's Dina all over again.''

Amy's heart went out to this kindhearted woman who, she was aware, had been almost a mother to Dina. ''Yes, isn't she?'' Amy agreed softly, touching Mattie's arm in a gesture of sympathy. She wanted to say something comforting, but at that moment Chrissie stirred restlessly. Conversation was suspended until the little girl gave a long, deep sigh and settled back into a sound sleep. The two women tiptoed out of the room, leaving the door ajar so they could hear her if she woke up.

Once they were downstairs again, introductions were quickly accomplished. The plump, grandmotherly-looking woman and the balding man were neighboring ranchers Iris and Herb Kramer. A younger couple were introduced as Reese's foreman Will Adler and his wife Haley. Will was almost as tall as Reese, with a slow way of speaking and a solemn demeanor. Amy detected a twinkle in his eye that told her there was a lively sense of humor beneath that sober exterior.

Will's wife had an open, outgoing manner that immediately appealed to Amy. She felt that under different circumstances she and Haley could easily become good friends. She reminded herself, though, that it wouldn't be a good idea to form any close attachments among these likable people while she was here. She couldn't take a chance on giving away the truth about her marriage to Reese. Besides, she felt guilty at the thought of accepting their friendship under false pretenses. What would they think of her if they found out what a fraud she was?

Drew Hammond, a distinguished-looking, graying man,

and his daughter Francine completed the group. Drew was also a rancher, and Francine ran a real-estate business in Red Deer. Although Francine's welcoming smile was cordial enough, there was something about the tall, slender blonde that made Amy slightly uncomfortable. She wondered if Francine might possibly have tagged Reese as her own property. If that was the case, she could have him back in a few months, Amy thought.

Once the introductions were completed, Iris spoke up. "We promise we won't stay late, honey—just long enough to toast the bride and groom and have some wedding cake. We know you're anxious to be alone."

"Now, Iris, you're going to embarrass them," her husband chided.

Iris waved away his teasing admonishment. "And why shouldn't they want to be alone? Just because *you're* an unromantic old stick-in-the-mud—"

"Herb, unromantic?" Drew echoed, his tone incredulous. "Why, Iris, just last week he took you to that livestock auction over in Randall. If that's not romantic, I don't know what is."

This remark was followed by a burst of laughter from the other guests. Amy gathered, from the lighthearted banter and the warm, easy camaraderie that flowed among these people, that they'd all been friends for so long that they were entirely comfortable with one another. She felt a pang of regret that she wouldn't be here long enough to become a part of their close-knit little group.

"Hey, we gonna have some wedding cake," Will asked, "or are we gonna stand around and shoot the breeze about how romantic ol' Herb is?"

As everyone seconded the idea of refreshments, the women laughingly hustled Amy to the table so she could cut the first piece of cake. Before handing the beribboned knife over to Amy, Haley deftly slid it under the small top layer with the bride and groom figures on it, and lifted it off. Placing it on a plate, she set it to one side. ''We'll wrap this and put it in the freezer,'' she said. ''You're supposed to save it, you know, so you and your husband can eat it on your first anniversary.''

Amy hoped nobody noticed the sudden flush that stained her cheeks. A year from now this marriage would be nothing but a memory. She stole a look at Reese to see what his reaction was to Haley's remark. Except for a brief shadow that darkened his features and was gone so quickly it could have been a trick of the light, there was nothing to indicate he'd even heard it.

She turned her attention to the cake. As she poised the knife over it, ready to make the first cut, a voice called out, ''Smile!'' Glancing up to see who had spoken, she was temporarily blinded by the sudden burst of light from a flash camera. She was so startled her hand slipped, causing her to demolish one of the roses.

''There,'' Herb said with a satisfied nod, as she tried to blink away the little pinpoints of light dancing before her eyes. ''I'll give you a copy when I get the roll developed. Years from now, when you and Reese are an old married couple, you'll have something to remind you of when you came here as a new bride.''

When everyone had been served a piece of cake and a cup of punch, Mattie said, ''We should toast the bride and groom.'' She turned to Drew. ''Would you do the honors?''

''I'd be happy to.'' With a courtly gesture, he raised his cup. ''May your love withstand the test of time. May it become stronger with every passing year.'' With his deep, resonant voice, he sounded as if he were pronouncing a benediction on them.

As Amy took a sip of punch, her glance met Reese's

over the rim of her cup. She wondered if he felt as guilty as she did, deceiving these well-meaning people. As usual, it was impossible to tell, from his expression, what he was thinking.

True to their promise, the guests began to say their good-byes before long. Amy wasn't sure whether to be relieved or sorry the party was breaking up so early. True, having to put on an act for all these people had been an ordeal. It paled in comparison, though, to what she would have to face after they left.

Mattie would have to know the truth, of course.

As for the others ... Amy realized she hadn't thought that far ahead. She supposed she'd had some vague idea that Reese led such a solitary life there would be few people around who would be interested in his affairs. She'd formed a mental picture of him as aloof and withdrawn, dedicated to running his ranch with a single-mindedness that left him little time or inclination for a social life.

Obviously, she'd been wrong. From the conversation that had flowed around them tonight, she'd gathered that his unexpected marriage was the talk of the entire valley.

In one respect, it would be a relief if those in Reese's inner circle of friends could be told the truth. At least then she and Reese would be spared having to put on an act in front of them. She realized, though, that the less these people knew about the situation, the better. Stanly Bender didn't take defeat easily, and she wouldn't put it past him to come snooping around, asking questions. They simply couldn't take the chance that one of Reese's friends might inadvertently give away some bit of information that Stanly could use to have the custody decision overturned.

No, she and Reese were going to have to go on pretending when other people were around.

But they couldn't pretend in front of Mattie.

Everything in her shrank from revealing their deception to the housekeeper. She toyed with—and quickly discarded—the idea of simply not telling her. With the three of them living in the same house, Amy realized how difficult it would be for her and Reese to keep up the charade.

Once the last of the guests had left, Mattie turned to Amy and Reese and said, "I know you've both had a long day. Why don't you go on up to bed and I'll straighten up down here and turn the lights out."

This was it. The moment of reckoning. They couldn't put it off any longer.

All at once Amy felt incredibly weary. The long trip and the strain of the past few weeks were starting to take their toll on her. And finding herself the guest of honor at a surprise party celebrating a marriage that wasn't a real marriage at all hadn't helped. She just wanted to go to bed. She shot Reese a look that almost shouted, *Tell her!*

Mattie glanced from Reese to Amy, and back to Reese. Clearly, she sensed there was something in the air. "Now then, what's going on here?" she demanded.

Reese looked uncomfortable. "Wh-what do you mean?"

"I had a feeling the minute you two walked in tonight that something wasn't quite right, but I couldn't say anything with the others around. Maybe it's none of my business, but I can't stand by and watch you get your marriage off to a bad start. It's natural, you know, for couples—even newlyweds—to have disagreements sometimes. That's just part of being married." She fixed Reese with a stern look. "I don't know what you've done to this sweet girl, but you'd better make it right or you'll have to answer to me."

Up to now, Reese had withstood Mattie's lecture stoically, saying nothing in his defense, his expression growing more and more puzzled. Now he said, "Mattie—"

"I suspect you must have had some kind of little tiff on

the way out here,'' the housekeeper went on, determined
to have her say. ''That may be, but—''

''Mattie!''

Something in his voice caught her attention this time.
She waited to see what he had to say.

''Mattie, I explained in my phone call that this isn't a
real marriage. I mean, it *is*—that is, it's all legal. . . .'' His
words trailed off helplessly.

''The only thing I could be sure of from that call was
that you and Amy were married, and that you were bringing
her and the children home. After that, all I heard was static.
Apparently,'' she said dryly, ''there was something I
missed.''

''What I was trying to tell you over the phone,'' Reese
said, ''was that the reason we got married was so we could
get custody of the kids.''

Mattie's expression revealed nothing of how she felt
about this bit of information. ''Maybe you'd better start
from the beginning.''

Reese shifted his weight from one foot to the other as
he explained—haltingly—about how he and Amy had both
wanted custody of Kevin and Chrissie, and about Stanly
Bender. ''The lawyer said the fact that Stanly was married
could be the deciding factor in a custody hearing.''

''So you concocted this idea of getting married to each
other?''

Reese lifted one shoulder in a shrug that indicated he'd
had no choice. ''It was either that or take a chance on
Bender getting his hands on the kids. I've met this guy,
and believe me, he's not the person you'd want raising
Dina's kids.''

Mattie turned to Amy, giving her a searching look. ''And
you agreed to this?''

Amy flushed under the older woman's scrutiny. She

found herself wishing she were somewhere—*anywhere*—else. Now that this whole thing was out in the open, it sounded so . . . so *deceitful*.

She forced herself to meet Mattie's gaze, resisting the urge to look down at her hands. "I—I didn't see any other way of protecting Kevin and Chrissie. I'd do anything to keep Stanly from getting anywhere near them."

She hardly dared breathe as she waited to see what Mattie's reaction would be. Was she going to tell them that what they'd done was shameful, that they had desecrated sacred vows and that she wanted no part of this deception?

After what seemed a very long time, the housekeeper said, "You did what you had to do. I'd likely have done the same thing if I'd been in your situation." She turned her attention to Amy, giving her a long, searching look. "You look about done in. You'd better get to bed before you collapse."

"I'll go on up and take Amy's suitcases to the guest room," Reese said, disappearing up the stairs.

As Amy started after him, Mattie's voice followed her. "There's one thing Reese didn't make quite clear. What happens once you're sure this Stanly Bender has given up trying to get custody of the kids? Are you and Reese going to fight one another for them?"

Amy stopped, but didn't turn around. She swallowed to ease the lump in her throat before replying. Once she was sure she could trust her voice, she said, "Reese convinced me they'd be better off with him. I—I'm willing to step aside and let him have them."

"And what about this marriage, or nonmarriage, or whatever it is?"

"We'll get a divorce or annulment—whichever is quickest and easiest."

"And then . . . ?"

"I'll go back to Seattle, or—or whatever."

As she continued up the stairs she heard Mattie say something under her breath. It sounded like, "What a pity."

Chapter Nine

Amy snuggled deeper under the covers, trying to shut out the screeching of a bird. Frowning, she pulled the blanket up over her head, but the shrill squawk still penetrated her sleep-fogged brain.

Something wasn't right.

Where were the traffic noises, the honking horns, the sirens in the distance, the usual sounds of Seattle waking up? A corny cliché from an old Western movie popped into her head: *It's too quiet out there.*

Except for that stupid bird.

"Go away," she muttered. Pushing a corner of the blanket to one side, she opened her eyes and peeked out. She closed them and retreated back under the covers as a shaft of bright sunlight nearly blinded her.

After a moment she opened them again, more cautiously this time. Her glance darted around the room, taking in the crisp white curtains at the window, the comfortable-looking rocking chair with a crocheted afghan lying over the back of it, the braided rug on the floor.

The last vestiges of sleep vanished. She wasn't in Seattle; she was at Reese's ranch. Throwing the blankets aside, she sat up in bed as the events of the night before came rushing back: the surprise party, the wedding cake with the bride and groom on top, Reese's friends wishing them a long and happy marriage.

After the strain of having to smile and put on an act, she'd been so keyed up she'd expected to toss and turn all night. Apparently, however, she'd fallen asleep the minute she hit the pillow. She hadn't slept so soundly since . . . well, since she'd taken over the care of the children.

The children! She'd intended to be up well before them, but she could tell by the angle of the sunlight slanting in the window that she'd slept later than she'd expected to. Kevin and Chrissie were likely already stirring. Shrugging into her robe, she hurried down the hall to their rooms. She didn't want them to be frightened at awakening in a strange place.

But the doors to both rooms were open, and their beds were empty. Her heart sank. They must have gotten up early, and were wandering around this big house trying to find her, probably crying. And what if they'd gone outside? There were all kinds of things on a ranch that could be dangerous to a small child—horses, tractors, and other pieces of machinery, maybe a large dog or two. Or they could wander off and get lost. She shuddered at the memory of the rocky, wooded terrain she'd seen last night on the way here. It would be almost impossible to find two small children in that wilderness. It was that thought that galvanized her into action.

She should never have agreed to bringing Kevin and Chrissie here, she thought as she flew down the stairs. Somehow, she could have found a way to care for them. Why hadn't she stood her ground and applied for custody herself, instead of allowing Reese to intimidate her into going along with his crazy scheme? This wild, hostile land, filled with hidden dangers, was no place to raise children.

She paused at the bottom of the stairs, trying to decide

what to do next. Maybe she should search the house before raising an alarm. On the other hand, though, if they *had* gone outside, the sooner she started looking for them the easier it would be to find them.

As she stood there trying to make up her mind, a voice drifted out to her from another part of the house. She couldn't make out the words, but it was definitely Kevin's high, childish treble. He didn't sound too alarmed, she noted with relief. But maybe that was because he was trying to calm his little sister, to reassure her that everything was all right, that Aunt Amy hadn't abandoned them.

Following the direction of his voice, she found herself in a large, sunny kitchen. Kevin and Chrissie were seated at the table, each with a bowl of cereal and a glass of milk in front of them. Both were attired in jeans, T-shirts, and their new boots, and Chrissie's flyaway curls were pulled back into a neat ponytail.

Kevin was explaining to Mattie, who was cutting biscuits and arranging them on a baking sheet, about his favorite television superheroes, a colorfully clad trio who went about righting wrongs and making the world a better place.

''See, they got their superpowers from this wizard named Vespar, but they had to promise to use them only for good. There's Troy—he can make people obey him if he rubs his ring and says the magic words. And Ariel can tell what people are thinking when she's wearing her pendant—''

He broke off when he spotted Amy in the doorway. ''Aunt Amy, guess what? Mattie—she's our new friend— says there are some kittens in the barn. When Uncle Reese comes back he's gonna take us out to see them. And then he said he'll take us for a ride around the ranch in the Jeep.''

Mattie glanced up from what she was doing and gave Amy a curious look. All at once she realized what a sight she must have made, bursting into the kitchen that way. She was uncomfortably aware of her disheveled appearance, of her hastily donned robe and her uncombed hair. Probably everyone around here had been up for hours, and had already done half a day's work.

Her relief at finding Kevin and Chrissie unharmed was tinged with guilt. She should have been up to look after them, instead of lying in bed. They could have wandered off and gotten lost or injured.

What must Mattie think of her? she wondered. Probably that she was too scatterbrained and irresponsible to be looking after young children, and that it was a good thing Reese had brought them here, where they could be properly cared for.

"I—I didn't mean to sleep so late," she murmured, pulling her robe around her and pushing a strand of hair out of her eyes.

"No reason why you shouldn't have." Mattie brushed the flour from her hands. "Last night you looked about done in. I told the children not to wake you up."

"Mattie said you needed to rest," Chrissie put in, "and we should be very, very quiet." Her ponytail bobbed up and down as she spoke.

"Now then," Mattie said, as she slid the pan of biscuits into the oven, "what can I fix you for breakfast?"

"I don't usually eat much in the morning. I'll just make myself a piece of toast or something later."

Mattie turned to face her, hands on her hips. "You'll do no such thing. If that's the way you always eat, it's no wonder you're nothing but skin and bones. What you need is some fattening up. You go upstairs and get dressed while I make you a proper breakfast. Now hurry. These biscuits will be done by the time you get back."

Amy started to protest, then changed her mind as the

tempting aromas floating around Mattie's kitchen reminded her that she really was hungry. Maybe it was the fresh air that was stimulating her appetite, or the fact that yesterday she'd been so nervous that her stomach had rebelled at the very thought of food. Even last night she'd eaten only a few bites of cake.

"How do you like your eggs?" Mattie called after her as she started up the stairs.

"Over easy," she replied over her shoulder.

As she showered she recalled how frightened she'd been a few minutes earlier at discovering Chrissie and Kevin missing from their beds. Mingled with her relief at finding them in the kitchen with Mattie, perfectly content, was an undertone of something else she couldn't quite put into words.

She'd had some idea of turning them over to Mattie's care gradually, so they'd have a chance to become accustomed to this new person in their lives. They seemed to have already accepted her without reservation, though. Amy supposed she ought to be relieved that the transition was being accomplished so easily.

Still, she couldn't suppress a little pang of emptiness at the realization that she could be so easily replaced in the children's affections.

She reminded herself that her own feelings were of secondary importance to what was best for them. After all, the main reason she had decided not to oppose Reese in his plan to obtain custody of them was because she knew Mattie was better equipped to care for them than she was.

She hadn't expected it to hurt so much, though.

Mindful of Mattie's admonition to hurry, she dressed quickly, in denim jeans and a plaid cotton shirt. As she zipped the jeans up, she noticed how loose they were on her. Recalling Mattie's earlier remark about her being nothing but skin and bones, she had to admit she could use a few more pounds. She knew she hadn't been eating properly lately. Between the combined stress of losing her brother and her sister-in-law, and all the responsibilities that had suddenly fallen on her shoulders, eating had been the farthest thing from her mind.

By the time she returned to the kitchen, Kevin and Chrissie had finished eating and were playing in the spacious den. "You're just in time," Mattie said, bringing a steaming, napkin-wrapped basket to the table. "These biscuits are fresh from the oven. Why don't you get started on them while they're still hot."

As soon as Amy was seated Mattie placed a plate of perfectly cooked bacon and eggs in front of her and filled her coffee cup before busying herself at the counter.

As pleasant as it was to have breakfast served to her, Amy felt obligated to make some sort of objection. She didn't want the housekeeper to think she was nothing but a spoiled city girl who didn't intend to lift a finger. "Mattie," she said, twisting around in her chair, "please don't feel you have to wait on me. You have enough to do—"

Mattie silenced her protests with a succinct "Hush. I enjoy taking care of people." After a moment of hesitation, she added, "And you certainly look as if you could do with a little looking after." Her matter-of-fact tone and manner indicated the subject was closed to further discussion.

Well, she'd tried, hadn't she? Amy thought. If she protested too much, it might only cause hard feelings. She helped herself to a biscuit and lavishly spread it with butter and jam, aware that Mattie was watching her approvingly. She heard the older woman say something under her breath about, ". . . put some meat on you . . ."

As Amy ate, she reflected on what a novelty it was to have someone actually concerned about her, even in such a small matter as whether she was eating properly. She hadn't had the luxury of easing into adulthood gradually. It had been thrust on her before she was quite ready for it. It seemed she had been looking after herself for almost as long as she could remember.

The back door opened and Reese stepped into the kitchen. "Got anything around here for a hungry man to eat?"

At the sound of his voice Kevin and Chrissie ran in from the other room, rushing past Amy to throw themselves against him with enthusiastic abandon.

He nodded a brief "Good morning" to Amy, as he swung Chrissie up into his arms. "Did you sleep well?"

"Like a log," Amy replied. "At least until—"

She had intended to say something about how she'd been momentarily disoriented by the lack of traffic sounds, but Kevin broke in with, "Uncle Reese, can we go for our ride now?"

Reese turned his attention to the boy. "Sure, sport, in a few minutes. Just let me get something to eat."

It occurred to Amy that once the barest of amenities had been observed, Reese apparently felt that was all that was required of him. Was he afraid that anything more than the most rudimentary display of interest might be misconstrued? Well, he needn't worry, she decided. She wouldn't dream of forcing her company on him.

While Mattie poured him a cup of coffee he scooped up a couple of biscuits with his free hand. "Some of the boys are moving part of the herd to the summer pasture," he said. "I thought I'd take the kids down and let them watch."

Amy realized, as the two children looked at one another in delight, that they were so eager to go with Reese they'd barely even glanced her way. She gave a philosophical shrug. How could she hope to compete with kittens, and real cowboys herding real cows?

She knew it wasn't just the kittens or the cattle, though. There was an undeniable something about Reese that drew others to him. She couldn't help noticing how the atmosphere in the room had changed with his arrival. He brought with him a subtle but unmistakable air of energy and vitality, of uninhibited good spirits. She could see why Kevin and Chrissie were so delighted to see him.

Now that he was back on his home ground, he seemed a different person from that serious, reserved stranger she'd first encountered in Seattle. She supposed he was glad to be home again, and pleased with himself because things had worked out according to his plans. He'd gotten custody of the kids, which was what he'd wanted. The only hitch was that it was a package deal, which included her. She was the one complication, the fly in the ointment. No doubt it would be a tremendous relief to him when the time came for them to put an end to this sham marriage so she could leave and he could get on with his life.

And did getting on with his life have anything to do with Francine Hammond?

Now where had *that* thought come from? she wondered.

Kevin tugged at Reese's hand. ''Come on.''

Reese drained his coffee cup. ''We're on our way.''

''You be careful with those children,'' Mattie called after him as the trio started out the door.

''Don't worry, I'll take good care of them,'' Reese promised.

Once they were gone Amy felt unaccountably let down. Since she was going to be living here for the next few months, she wouldn't have minded seeing some of the ranch. She hadn't been invited, though.

She told herself it was no big deal. If she'd wanted to

go along she should have spoken up. She couldn't expect Reese to be a mind reader. He was a busy man, with a ranch to run, and didn't have time to cater to her.

Still, he could have at least asked. Was this going to be his attitude the entire time she was here? she wondered. All at once she had the feeling she could leave today, and nobody would even miss her.

She tried to shrug off the dismal thought. Self-pity wasn't her style. Her sense of depression refused to be dispelled, though. Maybe it was because the reality of what she'd done hadn't actually begun to sink in until she'd seen Kevin and Chrissie in what was to be their new home. Already they were settling in as if they'd always lived here. They'd accepted Mattie without reservation, and of course they both adored Reese.

He'd said she'd be welcome to come and visit as often as she wanted, but she knew it wouldn't be the same. Reese would be the central figure in their lives, and she'd just be the aunt who dropped in from time to time. They probably wouldn't even think of her between visits.

It was too late to start having regrets, though. What was done was done.

She realized Mattie had approached with the coffeepot.

"Ready for a refill?" Without waiting for a reply, the housekeeper filled Amy's cup, then poured another cup for herself and sat down across the table from her. As she stirred her coffee, she regarded Amy thoughtfully.

"Those children really mean a lot to you, don't they?"

"Yes, they do. They're the only family I have left."

"How do you feel about turning them over to Reese?" Mattie asked bluntly.

Amy wasn't too surprised at the question. Even in the brief time she'd been there, she'd noticed that the older woman wasn't one to beat around the bush. "I didn't have

much choice,'' she replied. ''Reese convinced me they'd
be better off with him. He has much more to offer them
than I do. If I have to lose them, I'd rather it was to him
than to Stanly Bender. That's why Reese and I decided to
join forces to keep Stanly from getting them.''

''I admire what you're doing, but I don't mind telling
you I was disappointed when I found out your marriage to
Reese isn't real.''

Amy could think of no suitable reply to this remark, so
she simply waited for Mattie to continue.

''Honey, if any man ever needed a wife, it's Reese. He's
so busy looking after everyone else, he never takes any
time for himself. When he was at the age when he should
have been out having a social life, he had Dina to raise.
She was so broken up over losing her parents that he put
aside his own needs. By the time she was grown it seemed
he'd gotten out of the habit of thinking of himself. And
then there's this ranch. He's convinced he has to oversee
every detail of the ranch's operation. There are a lot of
people whose livelihoods depend on this place, and he feels
a real obligation to them.''

This was a side of Reese Amy hadn't seen. Oh, she'd
already noticed his tendency to take charge of a situation,
but she'd assumed it was because he had a controlling type
of personality, or that he was one of those people who were
sure nothing would be done properly unless they did it
themselves. Now she was beginning to realize that it
stemmed more from a sense of duty than from a need to
dominate everyone around him.

''It's time he quit worrying so much about other people
and started thinking about what's good for him,'' Mattie
went on, warming to her topic. ''What he needs is a woman
in his life. Not that he hasn't had plenty of chances. Used
to be a lot of women throwing themselves at him, until

most of them saw how much good it was doing. 'Course, there's still some that have their eye on him—not mentioning any names.''

Amy wondered if the older woman might be referring to Francine Hammond, but she refrained from asking.

Mattie gave her a speculative look. ''I don't suppose there's any chance . . .'' Her voice trailed off. ''No,'' she said resolutely. ''I'm not one to meddle in matters that don't concern me.''

Amy suppressed a smile. She had no doubt at all that Mattie would have no qualms whatever about meddling, if she felt it was in the best interests of those involved.

Once she had her clothes unpacked and put away, Amy found herself at loose ends. She'd offered to help with the household chores, insisting she didn't want to be treated like company, but Mattie had shooed her away with, ''Don't worry, there'll be plenty for you to do later. You're entitled to a day or so to get settled in.''

''Well, then,'' Amy said, ''I think I'll go out for a walk. I could do with some exercise.'' Actually, it wasn't exercise she needed as much as a chance to be alone, to sort out her feelings.

She tried to tell herself it was childish for her to have been hurt by Reese's barely cordial greeting. She certainly didn't expect him to play the part of attentive bridegroom when there were no outsiders around. On the other hand, though, she had thought they might at least observe the polite amenities.

She was beginning to realize this whole thing was going to be more difficult than she'd expected. She and Reese should have set some ground rules right from the start. She hadn't given any thought to the business of day-to-day living in the same house. If his attitude this morning was any indication, they apparently were to conduct themselves as polite strangers, maybe exchanging brief pleasantries if their paths happened to cross, and then each going on about his or her business.

Did the man consider himself so irresistible that he was afraid she might misinterpret any display of normal courtesy? If that was what was worrying him, she'd make sure she kept her distance.

As she stepped out the back door she paused to get her bearings. There were signs of activity around the barn and other outbuildings, and in her present state of mind she didn't feel up to meeting anyone. Skirting the area around the house, she found a trail that twisted and wound through tall trees.

In spite of her bleak mood, before long the fresh, pine-scented air, the cool breeze, and the sunlight filtering through the branches began to have a soothing effect on her. Her spirits lifted when she discovered a sparkling clear stream that meandered through a grassy field. When it disappeared into a thick stand of trees on the other side of the field, she quickened her step, eager to see where it went.

She was brought up short when she came to a sturdy fence bisecting the field. Hesitating, she scanned the area on the other side of the fence. The field seemed to be empty. She followed the fence until she came to a gate.

Chapter Ten

Reese was having the time of his life showing the kids around the ranch. Everything was new and exciting to them. He found himself looking at ordinary things in a different way, as Kevin chattered incessantly and asked a million questions, and Chrissie murmured little cries of delight as she knelt on the floor of the barn to let the kittens climb into her lap.

The only thing that stood in the way of his complete contentment was that little nagging feeling in the back of his mind, a sense of having left something undone.

He knew what it was, of course. He should have invited Amy to come along. He'd considered it. In fact, as he was ushering Kevin and Chrissie out the door he'd almost turned back to ask her if she'd like to come with them. He'd changed his mind, though, telling himself she probably wouldn't be interested in looking at a bunch of cows.

His conscience wouldn't let him off the hook that easily, though. Just before he'd left he'd caught a glimpse of something like hurt or disappointment in her eyes.

The truth was, now that he realized how attracted he was to her, he'd decided the wisest thing he could do would be just to keep his distance from her, so he wouldn't be

100

tempted to do anything foolish. Any kind of romantic involvement would only cause problems.

Still, his sense of duty prodded, he at least owed her common courtesy. He made up his mind that when he took the kids back to the house for lunch and naps, he'd invite Amy to come with him on a tour of the ranch.

Having come to this decision, he felt better. He'd show her some of the places of interest, help her to feel at home. Then, his obligation to her fulfilled, he could get back to his ranching duties with a clear conscience.

When he brought the kids in the back door, Mattie was at the counter making sandwiches. She sent Kevin and Chrissie off to wash their hands for lunch.

Reese glanced around the kitchen. "Where's Amy?"

"Not here," Mattie replied in clipped tones. "She went out for a walk."

She had her back to him, so he couldn't see her expression, but everything about her stance radiated disapproval. He wondered if it was directed toward him or Amy.

"I, ah, wish she'd waited," he said. "I was going to ask her if she wanted to take a tour around the ranch."

Mattie put the jar of peanut butter away, slamming the cupboard door with what seemed to be unnecessary force. He winced.

Mattie had worked for him long enough that he could tell when she was displeased about something, and it was obvious she was riled up at the moment. He wasn't sure what he'd done to get into her bad graces, but he had no doubt he was about to find out. Although his instinct for self-preservation told him to back out of the kitchen and head for the barn or some other safe haven with all due haste, he knew he'd eventually have to face her ire, so he might as well stay here and take it like a man.

Mattie whirled around to face him. ''You could have invited her along when you took the kids out.''

''If she wanted to go, why didn't she just say so?''

The housekeeper glared at him, hands on her hips. ''You certainly didn't give her any reason to think you wanted her company. You barely even said good morning to her.''

''It's not as if we were really husband and wife,'' he reminded her. ''You know the only reason we got married was so I could get custody of the kids.''

''And now that you've gotten what *you* want, you expect her just to quietly fade into the woodwork?''

He hoped that was a rhetorical question and didn't require an answer, because he didn't want to admit that was pretty much what he'd had in mind. He was spared having to reply as Kevin and Chrissie returned, holding their hands up for Mattie's inspection. While she was occupied with getting their lunch on the table he made a hasty exit.

He was scowling as he climbed back into the Jeep. His movements quick and angry, he put the vehicle in gear and sped out of the yard with a squeal of tires that caused several of the hands who were working nearby to glance at him curiously.

He didn't have time for all this game-playing, he told himself. He'd been away from the ranch too long, and there were a lot of matters that needed his attention. He pushed aside the thought that he had a good, reliable foreman who was perfectly capable of keeping things running smoothly in his absence.

He slowed down when he came in sight of the fenced pasture where Ranger, the bull he'd bought shortly before he left for Seattle, was confined. He wondered if the brute had calmed down any by now. Although the animal had good bloodlines, he had to admit he'd never seen such a worse-tempered beast.

"What—" Someone was in the pasture. His brow furrowed into a frown as he brought the Jeep to a halt. What kind of idiot would be out there strolling across the field as if he didn't have a care in the world? Everybody on the ranch had been cautioned to keep their distance from Ranger.

"Hey, get out of there!" he yelled.

The figure halted and glanced around. Who *was* that? It looked too small to be one of his hands. But there wasn't any other ranch within walking distance. He put the Jeep into gear and stepped on the gas.

As he drew close enough to recognize the slender figure, his heart slammed against his ribs. It was Amy! As soon as the Jeep was alongside the fence, he screeched to a halt.

He could see the huge animal at the far end of the field, as it lowered its massive head and pawed the ground, bellowing a warning. Although he couldn't make out Amy's features from this distance, it wasn't difficult to tell exactly the moment she became aware of the danger she was in.

It was amazing how fast such a large animal could move. "Get out of there!" he called again.

He muttered under his breath as Amy glanced toward the gate, then broke into a run. She wasn't going to make it in time. The fence was too high for someone her size to climb over quickly, and by the time she got the gate open Ranger would be breathing down her neck. He could almost see her slight form being tossed into the air on those sharp horns.

The appalling image spurred him to action. Standing up in the Jeep, he vaulted over the fence, then cut across a corner of the field, praying he wouldn't be too late. Already he could hear the pounding of hooves as the animal drew closer.

He reached Amy scant seconds before the bull did. Grabbing her around the waist, he almost threw her over the fence, then scrambled after her as Ranger stopped short and shook his head in anger.

While Reese lay on the ground on the other side, waiting for his heart to quit thudding, the huge beast paced back and forth, glaring at them through the fence. When he was finally able to breathe normally, he hoisted himself to his feet and extended a hand to Amy to help her up.

"What were you doing out there?" he demanded.

At his tone, she recoiled as if she'd been struck. He felt a twinge of guilt. After the close call she'd just had, the last thing she needed was someone yelling at her, but, doggone it, the realization that she could have been killed fueled his anger.

"This is a working ranch, not some kind of amusement park," he shouted. "You can't just go wandering around where you don't belong."

At his tone, her first reaction seemed to be stunned disbelief. She recovered quickly, though. "How was I to know there was a dangerous animal out there?" she shot back, her eyes flashing fire. "I'm not a mind reader, you know."

"You could have waited for me to show you around and point out the hazards, before going off on your own."

"And what am I expected to do in the meantime? Mattie has already taken over looking after the kids, and she wouldn't allow me to help with the housework. Am I supposed to put myself in a state of suspended animation. . . ." Her words trailed off and she emitted a little cry of alarm as Ranger rammed his head against the fence one last time, as if warning her that the next time she might not get away from him so easily.

Reese noticed how pale she had become. The term *delayed shock* came to mind. All the color seemed to have drained from her face.

He caught her just as her knees started to buckle. A pang of alarm shot through him as she went limp in his arms.

As the swirling gray mist that had clouded Amy's vision began to dissipate, she was vaguely aware that it was extremely pleasant to be held this way, supported by a pair of strong arms, her cheek resting against a broad chest. She could hear his heart beating against her ear. . . .

Good heavens, what was she doing?

She had no idea what had caused that sudden, momentary weakness. It must have been the memory of those pounding hooves and sharp horns, of the mean little eyes and hot, angry breath. At the time she was being chased, all her energy had been focused on simply getting away from the animal. It wasn't until the danger was past that she had time to realize how much harm he could have done to her.

But that was no excuse for fainting, like . . . like the heroine in a Victorian novel. Not more than twenty or thirty minutes ago she'd vowed to keep her distance from Reese, and here she was falling into his arms.

Struggling to throw off the lassitude that had taken control of her body, she flattened her hands against Reese's chest and tried to push away from him. It was a halfhearted effort, though, and when his arms tightened around her almost imperceptibly and he whispered, ''No, just stay here,'' she didn't have the strength to protest. As he patted her shoulder soothingly and murmured little words of comfort, she abandoned the attempt and relaxed against him, as if she could absorb some of his strength.

She knew she shouldn't be doing this. It was just

that . . . well, it had been a long time since she'd had anyone to lean on, and he felt so dependable, so sturdy and
reliable, so *good*. In just a few moments, when her legs
didn't feel quite so weak—

She was roused out of her lethargy by the sound of hoofbeats, accompanied by several voices. Glancing up, she saw
three men approaching on horseback. This time Reese
didn't try to stop her as she pulled away. They broke apart
as if they'd both touched something hot.

The trio reined their horses to a halt and dismounted.
''We seen you out showing your missus around the ranch,''
one of the men spoke up. He was short and stocky, with a
tanned, leathery face. ''Thought we'd ride over and say
howdy to the new Miz Cavanaugh.''

Howdy? Amy thought. *Did he really say ''Howdy''?*

''We wouldn't be interrupting anything, would we?'' a
second rider asked. Although his tone and demeanor were
serious, he winked knowingly, and nudged one of his com-
panions. He was younger than the other two, hardly more
than a boy, actually, and was tall and rail-thin.

Amy flushed slightly, as she realized they thought they'd
come upon a romantic moment between their boss and his
new wife. She wondered what they'd have thought if they'd
heard him yelling at her a few moments ago.

''We been looking forward to meeting you, ma'am,'' the
short, stocky man put in. ''I'm Jake.'' He tipped his wide-
brimmed hat in a courtly gesture. ''Mighty pleased to make
your acquaintance.''

''I'm glad to meet you too,'' Amy murmured, accepting
the large, callused hand he extended.

Not to be outdone, the third member of the trio stepped
up. ''They call me Curly. Never could figure out why.''
With a grin, he removed his hat, revealing a bald, shiny
pate.

"Marty's the name," the tall, skinny one said.

As Amy acknowledged the introductions, she had the unreal feeling that she'd stumbled onto the set of a Western movie. Any minute now, she expected to hear something like, "You must be the new schoolmarm, ma'am."

Once the ice was broken, the three cowhands almost elbowed one another out of the way in their eagerness to make her feel welcome.

"Hope you're going to like it here."

"If there's anything you need, just say the word."

"Be glad to show you around."

Reese had been watching this exchange without saying anything. Finally, with a slight frown, he asked, "Don't you boys have some work to do?"

"We better be getting back on the job," Marty said, obviously unintimidated by Reese's pointed remark. He couldn't resist a parting shot as he climbed back on his horse. "I expect you and your missus are wanting to be alone."

As the trio rode away, Reese said, shaking his head, "The boys laid it on pretty thick, didn't they? I hope they didn't overwhelm you."

"No, I thought they were very sweet."

Reese's lips twisted in a wry grin. " 'Sweet' isn't exactly the word I'd use."

He shifted his weight from one foot to the other, as if he had something to say, but didn't quite know how to go about it. "Ah, look, I'm sorry I yelled at you like I did, but . . . well, when I saw that bull coming at you it scared the daylights out of me."

Amy was still shaky from her close encounter with Ranger, and the unexpected apology caused sudden tears to prick her eyelids. She was afraid if she tried to speak her voice would break.

"I didn't mean I expect you just to stay in the house the whole time you're here," he went on. "Just please be more careful. Come on, I'll show you around the place, so you'll know where it's safe to go."

He put a hand around her waist and guided her toward the Jeep. As she walked along beside him, she was acutely conscious of his touch through the thin material of her shirt.

Chapter Eleven

"Well, aren't you the pretty thing," Amy murmured to the little mare.

In the few weeks she'd been here, she was gradually learning her way around the ranch. Today's exploration had brought her to the corral behind the barn, where several horses eyed her curiously. One, a fine-boned gray with large, intelligent eyes, ambled over to the fence.

Although Amy's recent encounter with Ranger had left her somewhat leery of anything much larger than a cocker spaniel, she had to admit this animal didn't seem very threatening. Tentatively, she slipped her hand through the bars and allowed the mare to nuzzle her fingers.

"Friends?" she asked, stroking the velvety muzzle.

The horse nickered softly, as if in response.

"Looks like you and Smoky are hitting it off real well."

Amy turned to see Jake, his arms resting on the corral fence, one booted foot on the bottom rail, watching her. "Living on a ranch, you'll be needing a horse for your own use. I'd suggest Smoky here." He gestured toward the mare. "She was included with several other horses the boss bought a while back, but she's actually a little too classy for ranch work. She'd be perfect for you. Has a lot of spirit, but she handles easy. 'Course, the boss might already have plans for getting you a horse.''

"Ah, no, I don't think he does. We—we haven't discussed it.'' She was on the verge of telling Jake she wouldn't need a horse of her own, since she wouldn't be here very long, but she caught herself just in time. She couldn't let him know she was only here temporarily.

" 'Course, you're welcome to the use of any of the horses on the place,'' Jake went on. "I wouldn't recommend your riding that one over there, though.'' His glance indicated a tall, rangy buckskin on the other side of the corral.

Amy studied the animal. He looked fairly harmless. "Is there something the matter with him?''

"Well, that depends on how you look at it. Actually, Pete's one of the best cutting horses we got, when he's being handled by someone who knows what he's doing. The thing is, he don't like being ridden by anyone who ain't had much experience. He has his own way of getting rid of them.''

"He bucks them off?''

"Well, not exactly. I've never known him to throw a rider. What he does is take them under a tree with low-hanging branches. Or if he can't find a tree, he runs them up against a bush. Brushes them right out of the saddle. He does it real gentle-like, but he makes his point.''

"You mean he does it on purpose?''

Jake nodded, chuckling. "I've seen other horses with the same bad habit, but none that had it down to a science the way ol' Pete does.''

"Why do you keep a horse like that around?''

"Well, like I said, he's a good cutting horse. We just have to be careful who rides him. Anyway, if it's all right with you, why don't we consider Smoky to be yours? I'll spread the word to the boys that she's for your personal use.''

''Smoky will be perfect,'' Amy said, smiling.

Jake looked pleased. ''Let's go look in the tack room and see if we can find you a good saddle and bridle.''

As Amy accompanied him into the barn, she felt a little pang of guilt. She didn't like deceiving all these nice people. The whole thing had gone too far for her to back out now, though.

Jake rummaged around in a room at the end of the wide corridor that divided the barn, and came up with a saddle that didn't look quite as large and unwieldy as some of the others. ''This one's about the right size for a lady,'' he said. ''Once I give her a good working over with saddle soap she'll look like new.''

''Oh, you don't have to,'' Amy protested. ''I can—''

''No trouble at all, ma'am. Glad to do it.''

There went that guilty feeling again. It was becoming all too familiar.

''Anybody around?'' a female voice called out.

Amy couldn't be sure, but she thought she detected a look of annoyance on Jake's leathery features. ''We're in here, Miz Hammond.''

A few seconds later, Francine appeared. The tan, Western-cut slacks and cream-colored shirt she wore set off her tall, slim figure to perfection. A square of what appeared to be real silk was knotted at her throat, and hardly a speck of dust marred the polished perfection of her boots. Not one wisp of her smooth, silvery-blond hair was out of place.

Next to her, Amy felt grubby and awkward. Her hair was tousled from roughhousing with Kevin and Chrissie, and she knew there were smudges of chocolate icing on her jeans from wiping her hands on them after frosting a cake for Mattie.

"I was looking for Reese," Francine said, glancing around. "Mattie said she thought he was in the barn."

"He ain't here." Jake offered no other information.

"Oh." Her disappointment was obvious. "I'll catch him later, then."

As Francine started to turn away, Amy felt a flush of resentment. Maybe the slight was unintentional, but she didn't think so. She told herself it didn't matter, since she and Reese weren't *really* husband and wife, except on paper. But it did matter. She didn't like being treated as if she were unimportant.

"Is there a message I can give *my husband?*" she asked sweetly, emphasizing the last two words.

For just a second, Amy could have sworn Francine's expression hardened. The hostile look was gone so quickly she could have imagined it, to be replaced by a smile that might or might not have been genuine. "It's nothing important, really. I just wanted to let him know that Dad is going over to Lowell next week to look at some stock, and he mentioned Reese might want to go along. I'm on my way home from town, and since I had to drive right by here anyway, I thought I'd just drop by and let him know."

"I'll tell him," Amy promised, resisting the urge to point out that she did have the intelligence to be trusted to relay a simple message.

If Francine caught a touch of sarcasm in Amy's tone, she covered it well. "Thank you," she replied, her poise unruffled.

"Well, I can't stand around here all day jawing," Jake said. "I got work to do." With that, he turned and left. As he reached the open doorway at one end of the barn, he almost collided with Reese. "Howdy, boss," he said in a growl, continuing on his way.

"What was that all about . . . ?" Reese started to ask, staring after Jake's retreating form. His words trailed off, and he glanced warily from Amy to Francine as if he had just sensed an undercurrent of tension in the air.

Francine waved one perfectly manicured hand in a dismissive gesture, as if to indicate it was nothing worth discussing. Stepping up to Reese, she put a hand on his arm.

Amy found herself fighting back a surprising urge to snap, *Take your hand off my husband.*

The gesture could have been nothing more than a sign of familiarity between two people who had known one another for a long time, she reminded herself. Her instinct told her, though, that the seemingly innocent act was carefully calculated to remind her that *she* was the outsider, the one who didn't belong here.

"I just dropped by to let you know Dad's going over to Lowell next week to look at that stock he told you about. He thought you might want to go along."

"Thanks. Tell him I'd like to go."

"I'll do that."

With the message delivered, Amy expected the other woman to leave. Removing her hand from Reese's arm, Francine glanced from Reese to Amy, a little smile—one reminiscent of a cat stalking a canary—playing around her mouth. "If I didn't know better, I'd almost think the honeymoon is over already," she drawled.

Amy shot a look at Reese. Had they done something to give themselves away? But she could tell, from his puzzled expression, that he was as much in the dark as she was.

"After only a couple of weeks of marriage, you've already stopped giving your wife a hello kiss?" Francine's tone was amused. "That's no way to insure a long, happy marriage," she scolded lightly.

She turned her attention to Amy. "Someone should have warned you, most of the men around here are strong, silent, undemonstrative types. A gal could get pretty tired of waiting around for them to show a little romance. To most of them, a wife rates somewhere below their horse and their truck."

On that note, she made her exit.

Once the growl of a high-powered sports car signaled Francine's departure, Amy turned to Reese angrily. "Thanks a lot!" she burst out.

Reese blinked in surprise. "What did I do?"

"It's what you didn't do. How do you expect us to make people believe our marriage is legitimate if you pay more attention to your neighbor than to your wife?" she demanded.

"Hey, I didn't notice you doing anything to enhance the image," Reese said defensively.

"How could I?" she shot back. "Francine attached herself to you before I even had a chance to say hello. That was *after* she made me feel as if I were a total idiot who doesn't even have the brains to deliver a simple message. I had the feeling she expected me to bow and scrape."

"Oh, so that's what this is all about." A look of understanding came over his features. "I see you've had a dose of Francine's, ah, somewhat forceful personality. I'll admit, she does come on a little strong, but that's just her way. She doesn't mean to intimidate people. As a matter of fact, her father told me she hopes you and she can become good friends."

I'll bet, Amy thought.

Had there been a hidden meaning in Francine's amused remark about the honeymoon being over? she wondered.

Was she simply teasing, or did she suspect their marriage wasn't all it appeared to be? She realized she'd better watch her step around this woman.

"I think I've shown remarkable restraint in letting you have a couple of weeks to get settled in," Haley said, when she called a few days later to invite Amy over for lunch, "but I'm dying for us to get together."

"I'd love to, but, ah, I don't have a way to get there." That, at least, was true. All the ranch vehicles were in use at the moment.

The foreman's wife quickly brushed aside that excuse with, "I'm sure we can work that out easily enough."

In the end, it was arranged that Haley would come for her in a little while, and Reese would pick her up a few hours later when his duties took him in that direction.

It wasn't that Amy didn't want to accept Haley's invitation. In fact, she sensed that the lively, outgoing redhead was someone with whom she could become good friends. That was the trouble. Friends shared feelings and exchanged confidences. She couldn't take the chance of inadvertently revealing the truth about her marriage to Reese.

Besides, when the time came for her to leave here, it would be easier if she hadn't formed any close attachments. Saying good-bye to Chrissie and Kevin was going to be difficult enough without having to part with friends.

In the short time she'd been here she'd already had a number of visits and phone calls from Reese's neighbors and acquaintances who were eager to meet his new wife. She felt like the worst kind of fraud. Under other circumstances she would have been delighted that these warmhearted people were so willing to welcome her into their circle. She didn't want to accept their friendship under false pretenses, though.

*   *   *

"It's just so romantic, the way you and Reese fell in love, practically at first sight," Haley said to Amy as they lingered over after-lunch coffee in Haley's cozy kitchen. "He must have swept you right off your feet."

"Something like that," Amy murmured. But if she hoped she wouldn't be pressed for details of their whirlwind courtship, she was in for a disappointment.

"Well . . . ?" Haley prompted.

"Really, there's not much to tell. We—we just decided to get married."

"This is positively the most interesting thing that's happened around here in ages," Haley said. "We always thought of Reese as the ultimate confirmed bachelor."

"Surely there must have been other women in his life." Amy recalled what Mattie had said about a lot of women throwing themselves at him.

"Oh, he dated, of course. But he always managed to keep from becoming too involved with any one woman."

"Wasn't there ever anyone, ah, special?" Mattie had mentioned something about ". . . there's still some that have their eye on him . . ."

"We thought so for a while, but then—"

"Who was it?" Amy couldn't resist asking.

Haley hesitated before replying. "I probably shouldn't tell you this, but—well, you're Reese's wife. You have a right to know. It was Francine Hammond."

So her instincts hadn't been wrong. "Ah—how serious was it?"

Haley shrugged. "It depends on which one of them you're talking to. They've known each other most of their lives, and I think Francine had him staked out as her personal property from way back. As for Reese . . ." Her lips curved into a smile. "He was serenely unaware that she had plans for him—or, at least, he seemed to be. Of course, it could have been an act. With Reese, it's kind of hard to tell what he's thinking.''

That was a masterpiece of understatement, Amy thought. ''So what happened? Did she finally give up on him?''

''Not really. Oh, she pretended to, but I think she still had hopes that she'd eventually wear him down.''

This was something that hadn't occurred to Amy when she'd agreed to this arrangement, that there might be someone else in his life. One jealous, vindictive woman could easily derail the entire plan. ''She, ah, must not have been too pleased to hear about me.''

''There's not a whole lot she can do about it, is there?'' Haley grinned impishly. ''You're the one he's married to. I have to admit, I'm not too disappointed to see her get her comeuppance.'' She made a little face. ''I don't mean to sound so catty. I should be ashamed of myself.''

Amy noted, however, that she didn't look too repentant.

''I like Francine—most of the time,'' Haley went on. ''It's just that her 'queen bee' act can really get under a person's skin.'' She took a sip of her coffee. ''But I didn't invite you to lunch so we could talk about Francine Hammond. I want to hear all about you and Reese.''

Amy realized her hostess was looking at her expectantly.

''Come on,'' Haley coaxed. ''How about a few details? We lead a pretty quiet life out here in the sticks, you know. We have to get our excitement vicariously.''

What could she say? Amy wondered with dismay. She supposed she could make up some romantic story about how she and Reese had suddenly realized they were in love, but she already felt guilty enough about deceiving Reese's friends.

She was spared having to add to her list of transgressions by the sound of footsteps on the back porch. ''That'll be

Reese," she said, jumping up. "I'll let him in." Although she was relieved at the interruption, her relief was tinged with apprehension. This would be the first time she and Reese had been together in front of "outsiders" since her little outburst in the barn the other day, and she wasn't sure what to expect.

He seemed to fill up the small kitchen as he stepped inside. He nodded a greeting to Haley over Amy's shoulder, then looked down at Amy, a disarming grin cutting deep grooves in his lean, tanned cheeks.

"I missed you, darling," he said in a stage whisper. With his back to Haley, he wiggled his eyebrows up and down wickedly, and mouthed the words, "It's showtime."

Relax, she told herself. He was just playing a role for Haley's benefit. But when his arms came around her and he drew her close to him, every instinct she possessed warned her to pull away, to put as much distance as possible between herself and Reese. With Haley looking on, though, she was more or less trapped. Besides, hadn't she berated him for not playing his part as a happy newlywed convincingly?

Still, he didn't have to throw himself into the role quite so wholeheartedly, she thought as his lips began brushing hers, teasing, caressing. . . .

All right, she wanted to whisper, *you don't have to overdo it.* She couldn't utter a word, though, as he continued his leisurely assault on her senses. It was obvious that he was having his little bit of revenge by deliberately trying to coax a response from her.

For a brief second she gave herself up to the sensations he was awakening in her. For the moment, nothing else mattered.

Until she saw the gleam in his dark eyes, as if he found

the situation amusing. She was jolted back to earth with a thud. Who did he think he was, anyway—heaven's gift to women?

Aware that Haley was watching them with unabashed interest, Amy extricated herself from his embrace. "We— we'd better be going," she said, with what aplomb she had left. "Thanks for lunch."

"We'll get together again soon, for a long talk," Haley said to Amy, as she accompanied her guests to the door.

Neither of them had much to say on the drive home. Occasionally, Reese shot a wary glance in Amy's direction, but she continued to look straight ahead, her features expressionless.

He couldn't blame her for being angry. That little scene he'd just staged had been stupid and childish. He'd acted like a ten-year-old kid trying to prove that nobody was going to tell *him* what to do. Still smarting from Amy's reprimand about his not being romantic enough in front of others, he'd made up his mind that she wasn't going to be the one to call the shots around here. If she wanted romantic, well, by golly, that was what she'd get.

His little trick had backfired, though. When he'd kissed her that way, deliberately trying to elicit a response, he hadn't counted on his own reaction. Although he didn't want to admit it—even to himself—during those brief moments she'd been in his arms, he'd been as deeply affected as she had.

Now his conscience was beginning to nag at him, reminding him that he'd overstepped the bounds of their agreement. After all, this whole marriage scheme had been his idea, and Amy was putting aside her own wishes to help him achieve his purpose. It would serve him right if she got fed up with him and his childish games, and decided to give up the whole thing and head back to Seattle. He owed her a lot, and he'd darned well better not forget it.

Chapter Twelve

For a while after the incident in Haley's kitchen, Reese and Amy maintained a guarded truce, putting on their act of being loving newlyweds in the presence of others, and keeping a wary distance from one another the rest of the time.

Before long, though, Reese's conscience again began to bother him. He'd been so wrapped up in his own concerns that he hadn't given much thought to her feelings. He should have been making sure she knew how much he appreciated her sacrifice, instead of trying to prove he had the upper hand.

It would serve him right if she decided to get out of the whole mess and head back to Seattle. That might be better all around, he thought. This whole arrangement wasn't working out quite the way he'd envisioned it.

But if she did leave, Stanly Bender would likely get wind of it and renew his attempts to gain custody of the kids. Unless he wanted the whole plan to fall through, he'd better start doing his part to make it work.

Of course, the whole situation was complicated by the fact that he didn't dare let Amy know that the memory of how warm and soft her lips had been under his was creeping into his thoughts with increasing frequency. Or that he found himself thinking more and more about the way she'd felt in his arms. If she had any idea how attracted he was to her she'd likely turn tail and run.

But that was his problem, not hers. He ought to be mature enough to keep his emotions under control. It was up to him to set the tone for their relationship: businesslike, yet courteous and polite.

Although apologies didn't come easily for him, he resolved to do whatever was necessary to atone for his behavior.

In spite of his best intentions, though, he found that getting back into her good graces wasn't going to be easy. She seemed suspicious of his attempts to make amends. For instance, when he suggested she might like to accompany him as he made his rounds of the ranch, she gave him a long, searching look, as if trying to determine if he had some ulterior motive in mind.

He felt uncomfortable under her scrutiny, mostly because he knew it was his own fault that she didn't trust him. Just when he'd decided she wasn't going to accept his invitation, she inclined her head slightly and replied, "I'd like that."

"Great." He was surprised at the rush of relief he felt that she hadn't turned him down flat. He eyed her canvas sneakers. "You'll need some boots for riding. Oh, and a hat to keep the sun off. We've got all kinds of stuff around the house. See what Mattie can fix you up with."

When she presented herself in the barn the next morning, properly attired in well-worn boots and a wide-brimmed Western hat, he nodded approvingly. With Mattie's help, she looked as if she'd lived all her life on a ranch.

As he made his rounds, Amy by his side, he explained about the business of raising cattle. She asked a lot of questions and appeared genuinely interested in the day-to-day operation of the ranch. She seemed to be enjoying the outing so much that Reese was a little ashamed that he hadn't thought to ask her to come along sooner.

When they returned late that afternoon and were seeing to the needs of their horses, Amy said, "I had a nice time today, Reese. Thanks for asking me." She tossed a ration of hay into Smoky's stall, gave him a final pat, and turned to leave the barn.

"You're welcome to go along anytime you want to, you know," Reese called after her. As he watched her walk away, he couldn't help admiring the way her slight figure was silhouetted in the late-afternoon sun that slanted in through the wide double doors.

Once the ice was broken Amy began accompanying Reese two or three days a week. Before long, "the boss and his lady" riding side by side became a familiar sight to the ranch hands. "Looks like the boss picked a winner," one of them commented to his coworker.

Amy didn't chatter the way some of the women of his acquaintance did, Reese noticed. Oh, they occasionally made light conversation but, just as often, they rode in companionable silence. It struck him that she was pleasant to have around—sort of restful.

Despite her big-city upbringing, she seemed to be taking to ranch life as if she'd been born to it. Although Reese hadn't expected her to help with the ranch chores—that wasn't why he'd invited her along—he noticed she didn't mind lending a hand when there was work to be done, whether it was mending fences or chasing down a cow that had strayed too far from the herd. On one occasion, when they came to a water hole that was clogged with brush and debris, she had no hesitation about pitching in to help clear it. When Reese pointed out that it was a muddy, dirty job, and she might want just to stay back out of the way, she shot him a look. "We have mud in Seattle too," she said.

Another time, they found a calf that had been born late in the season and had become separated from or been abandoned by its mother. The animal was almost too weak even to bawl.

"He'll have to be hand-fed," Reese said, hoisting the pathetic-looking creature over his saddle. "Probably won't do much good, though." He shook his head regretfully. "He's pretty far gone, and it'll take a lot of effort to get him back on his feet. I hate to have any of the boys take time out from their other work to play nursemaid to one calf."

"I could do it."

"You?" Reese gave her an appraising look.

"I realize I don't have any experience at this sort of thing, but surely it doesn't take any special knowledge, does it?" She sounded somewhat defensive.

"It's not that I don't think you could handle it. I just want to make sure you realize what you'd be getting into. It'll keep you pretty busy. He'll need to be fed several times a day for a while."

"It isn't as if I have all kinds of important things to do," she pointed out. "As it is, I feel like a fifth wheel around here. I might as well be doing something useful. Please let me try."

"All right, if you're sure you want to. But—well, just don't feel too bad if he doesn't make it."

In a short time the calf was bedded down in a stall in one corner of the shed next to the barn, and Reese showed Amy how to mix the milk substitute. She took her new responsibility seriously, patiently coaxing the frail animal to take the rich, nourishing liquid.

*   *   *

A week or so after Amy took on the job of looking after the orphaned calf, Reese awoke in the middle of the night and noticed, from his bedroom window, a light in the shed. Was someone prowling around out there? he wondered. Dressing quickly, he went down to investigate. The weather had turned unseasonably cold, and a blast of chilly air hit him as he stepped outside.

He approached the small structure cautiously and pushed the door open, a frown creasing his forehead. His features relaxed into an indulgent smile when he saw Amy sitting on the floor of the shed, her back resting against the wall, sound asleep. The calf was huddled up as close to her as possible, as if to share her body heat.

"What—" Her eyes flew open as Reese touched her shoulder gently.

"What are you doing out here?" he asked.

"I—I was worried about the calf. It's so cold tonight."

"He'll be all right. Come back to the house. You can't stay out here."

He helped her to her feet, and she stumbled sleepily out of the shed. As they started across the yard he noticed she was shivering. Although his first instinct was to wrap his arms around her to warm her up, he caught himself. Instead, he draped his jacket around her shoulders. It was so long it hung almost to her knees, giving her a waiflike appearance.

Keeping one arm around her shoulder, he guided her into the house and up the stairs. When they reached her bedroom, she leaned back against the door, still half-asleep.

As he stood looking down at her in the dimly lit hallway, he felt a rush of—he wasn't sure what to call it. Tenderness? Putting a finger under her chin, he tilted her face up and kissed her lightly on the forehead. Then he reached behind her for the doorknob and opened the door. ''Go to bed,'' he whispered, giving her a gentle nudge.

''There,'' Mattie said as she stood back and admired the gleaming jars of vegetables she and Amy had just put up.

''I know it's a lot of work, but we'll be glad we did it when we open some of those jars this winter. Those vegetables will taste good with Thanksgiving dinner.''

''Mattie—'' Amy began, then broke off with a little shrug.

Although Mattie didn't appear to have noticed Amy's aborted protest, Reese, who had come in for his usual mid-morning break, did. Likely, Amy had started to remind Mattie that she wouldn't be here by Thanksgiving, but then had given it up as a lost cause. For reasons known only to herself, the housekeeper had chosen to ignore the fact that Amy was only here temporarily. She became conveniently hard of hearing anytime the subject came up.

As Reese leaned casually against the counter, coffee mug in hand, he watched Amy without appearing to do so. Unaware that she was being observed, she let her guard down for just a second or two, allowing her expression to reveal a wistful sadness.

He'd noticed that look at other times, when she didn't realize anyone was watching her. Each time, it nagged at the edges of his conscience, causing a little stir of discomfort in him.

When he'd conceived this plan he'd been so sure he was doing the right thing, that this was his only possible course of action. He'd have custody of his niece and nephew, and they'd be raised in a stable, secure home. Everybody would benefit—except Amy.

But it was too late to start having regrets. There was no

other way he could have made sure Stanly Bender wouldn't get his hands on Kevin and Chrissie.

Besides, even if Bender hadn't been in the picture, Amy would never have been able to care for the kids on her own, despite her best intentions. She'd wear herself out trying to look after them and still make a living, and the kids would be shuttled back and forth between sitters and day-care centers. That wasn't the way Dina would want her children to be raised.

He didn't want Amy to be hurt, but he didn't see what else he could have done.

Amy sensed Reese's gaze on her. She felt self-conscious, knowing he was watching her. Even though they'd suspended hostilities and had settled into a comfortably casual friendship, she had no doubt it would be a tremendous relief to him when it was safe for them to end their sham marriage so she could return to Seattle and he could get on with his life.

She supposed she ought to be looking forward to getting on with her own life too. It was just that—well, there wasn't much for her to go back to, with Mike and Dina gone and Kevin and Chrissie now in Reese's care. Oh, she still had friends in Seattle, but that wasn't the same as family.

But this was no time to be thinking such dismal thoughts, while Reese was looking at her that way. "If you don't need me for a while, I'm going to run into Red Deer," she said to Mattie. "I need to do some shopping. I'll be back in time to look after Kevin and Chrissie so you can go to your deacons meeting at church."

"Of course, dear," the housekeeper replied. "Thanks so much for all your help."

Reese finished his coffee and set the cup on the counter. "Want me to drive you?"

"Thanks, but I can handle it. Don't forget, I'm used to Seattle traffic." She'd been into Red Deer several times, and was becoming familiar with the town and the twisting, winding back roads that led into it. Still, she appreciated the offer. It sounded almost . . . protective.

She turned to Kevin and Chrissie, who were having milk and cookies at the table. "Would you like to go into town with me?"

After brief consideration, Kevin shook his head. "Marty's gonna take me riding pretty soon."

"Me too," Chrissie piped up. "I get to go riding too."

Amy smiled understandingly. Naturally, going riding took precedence over a trip into town. Both children had their own ponies now. Chrissie's was a small, docile Shetland that seldom moved faster than a sedate walk. She was content to sit astride his back and be led around the barnyard by Reese or one of the hands.

Kevin, having turned five a few weeks earlier, had been deemed old enough for a "real" horse, and a small pinto was chosen for him. All of the hands on the ranch seemed to be trying to outdo one another in teaching him riding, roping, and other "cowboy stuff," as he put it, and he was proving to be an apt pupil.

As she gathered up her purse and car keys, Amy reflected on how well both children were adjusting to ranch life. Kevin was becoming less rambunctious, with so many outlets for his energy, and Chrissie was starting to get over her shyness and become more outgoing.

Oh, they still missed their parents, of course—sometimes she detected a wistful expression in Kevin's eyes, or sensed a sadness in the little girl, but that was to be expected.

Although it sent a pang of sadness through Amy to think about going away, she knew that when the time came she would be leaving Mike and Dina's children in good hands.

Both Reese and Mattie would do anything in the world for them.

As she maneuvered the Bronco into a parking spot on Red Deer's one and only main thoroughfare, several people who were passing by waved or greeted her by name.

Her first stop was the post office to buy stamps and mail some letters. Nate Bradly, the postmaster, asked how things were going out at the ranch, and if she was getting settled in all right. They chatted for a few minutes, and when Amy turned to leave she ran into Charlotte Hopkins, who asked, ''How's Kevin? I'm looking forward to having him in my class.'' Charlotte would be Kevin's teacher when he started kindergarten in a few weeks. Amy had met her when she and Kevin had gone to register him for the coming school year.

''He's fine. He can hardly wait for school to begin.''

As she continued on down the street after leaving the post office, Mrs. Bigelow, who ran the bakery, gave her a friendly wave through the window of her establishment and beckoned for her to come in.

''Got some fresh chocolate doughnuts,'' the plump, cheerful proprietor said as Amy entered the shop, causing the bell over the door to ring. ''Thought you might like to try one. The last time you were in you mentioned they're your favorites.''

Once she was back out on the street, after sampling Mrs. Bigelow's wares, she headed for the library, where the librarian greeted her with, ''That book you were looking for just came in. I put it aside for you.''

On her earlier trips into town, she'd been surprised at how many people knew who she was, let alone such bits of information as what her reading habits were, and that she liked chocolate doughnuts. Now she took it as a matter of course that everyone in Red Deer knew everyone else's business. At first she'd felt as if she were living in a fishbowl, but by now she'd decided it was kind of pleasant. It gave her a feeling of belonging.

She had one more stop to make. She needed to look for a dress to wear to a sort of barnwarming that was coming up this Saturday night. Iris and Herb Kramer, one of the couples she'd met her first night here, had just built a new barn and had decided to initiate it with a barn dance before it was put to use for its intended purpose.

''We'll be expected to be there, you know,'' Reese had said, sounding almost apologetic. Although it wasn't the most eloquent invitation she'd ever received, she realized he was simply pointing out that the townsfolk would think it odd if Red Deer's newest newlyweds didn't put in an appearance.

According to Mattie, Iris and Herb loved entertaining, and practically any occasion could be turned into an excuse for a party. Amy found she was kind of looking forward to going, although she was also a little nervous over the prospect. It would be the first time she and Reese attended a local social event as a couple, and she was sure they would be the subject of much interest.

As she'd surveyed the contents of her closet, it struck her that she didn't have anything suitable to wear. Although she wasn't sure exactly what the proper attire was for a barnwarming, she was fairly certain nothing in her wardrobe would fill the bill.

Now she stood on the sidewalk uncertainly, looking up and down the street. She had no idea which stores in Red Deer sold women's clothing, since she hadn't shopped for clothes since she'd been here. And she didn't have time to explore all the side streets if she intended to get home in time for Mattie to get to her meeting.

When she heard her name being called, she turned to see Haley rushing across the street toward her.

"Am I glad to see you," Amy greeted her with relief. "I need your help. I have to find something to wear to the Kramers' party. Where's the best place to buy clothes?"

"Sadie's has about the best selection in town. C'mon, I'll take you there," she said, linking an arm through Amy's chummily.

Sadie's was located on a side street just off the main thoroughfare. Once there, Haley threw herself into the search for the proper garment with enthusiasm. "This is going to be fun. We'll find you something a little extra-special," she said.

"Oh, no, I—I don't want anything fancy."

Haley waved her protests aside. "This is your unofficial introduction into local society. You might as well do it with flair."

But Amy vetoed several of Haley's selections. It wasn't that she had anything against dressing up in pretty clothes—but now that she and Reese were both aware there was a strong physical attraction between them, the last thing she wanted was to look as if she had gone to a great deal of trouble to impress him.

Besides, in view of the fact that their hasty marriage was already a topic of much speculation by Reese's neighbors and friends, she wanted to call as little attention to herself as possible.

She couldn't tell any of this to Haley, of course. Finally, shaking her head in feigned exasperation, Haley said, "Well, how about this one, then?"

Amy took a look at the simple, peasant-style dress Haley held out for her inspection. Full skirted, with an off-the-shoulder neckline, it was in her favorite shade of blue, with touches of silver trim. Taking the hanger from Haley, she held the garment up in front of her as she looked in the mirror. Glancing at her watch, she saw that she wouldn't have time to try it on if she intended to get back to the ranch in time for Mattie to get to her meeting. It looked to be about the right size, anyway.

"I'll take it," she said.

In her bedroom the night of the party, Amy took one last critical look at her reflection. She chewed her lower lip thoughtfully. On a hanger, the dress had looked fairly demure—almost prim, in fact. Now she wasn't so sure it had been a wise choice. It wasn't just that the full skirt and wide belt emphasized her slim figure, or the way that particular color made her eyes look bluer.

She hadn't realized the soft cotton material of the bodice would cling to her body in such a figure-revealing way, or that the off-the-shoulder neckline was quite so—well, so off-the-shoulder. She tried pulling it up, but it kept slipping back down.

She must have something else she could wear tonight, she thought, hoping Sadie's didn't have a no-return policy. But if she took the time to rummage through her closet and then change clothes she'd have to come up with some kind of explanation about what was taking her so long, and that would just complicate matters further.

Hesitantly, she started down the stairs, trying to quell the butterflies in her midsection. When she reached the middle landing and Reese came into view, her first glimpse of him almost caused her to forget her trepidation about her own attire. Clad in black Western-style jeans that molded his trim hips and thighs, and a black Western shirt trimmed with little touches of silver, he looked almost dangerously attractive.

He glanced up at her briefly. "I'm ready to go whenever

you are. . . .'' he began. His words trailed off and he did a sort of double take. He gave her a long, appraising look.

Amy's steps slowed almost to a halt. ''My dress—it's all wrong, isn't it? It'll just take me a minute to run up and change. I'm sure I can find something else—''

''No.''

The clipped monosyllable startled her into silence. When he spoke again there was a sort of husky quality in his voice. ''The dress is fine. It's more than fine. Don't change a thing.''

He didn't step aside when she reached the bottom of the stairs. He was so close she thought he must be able to hear the rapid beating of her heart, to sense that every cell in her body had leaped to sudden, vibrant life. As his eyes caught and held hers, everything around her faded into nothingness, as if they were the only two people in existence. . . .

The spell was broken as Chrissie bounded into the room. At the sight of Amy she came to a sudden halt, her eyes widening. ''Aunt Amy, you look just like a princess,'' she exclaimed in a voice tinged with awe. Her brother, for once speechless, simply stared, his gaze going from Amy to Reese and back again.

Fresh from their baths and clad in pajamas, both children were all pink and rosy. ''Mattie said we could stay up long enough to say good night,'' Kevin said when he regained his voice.

As Amy knelt to hug both children, she wasn't sure whether to feel relieved or disappointed at the interruption.

''My, it seems a shame to interrupt such a charming little domestic scene.''

A flash of irritation went through Amy as she recognized Francine's amused drawl. Every word grated on her like fingernails screeching down a blackboard. Glancing up over her shoulder, she saw that her fears were confirmed.

"There didn't seem to be anyone around to answer the door," Francine said, "so I let myself in. I hope you don't mind, but Reese and I have been friends for so long that we don't stand on ceremony."

After that incident in the barn a few weeks ago, when Francine had made those teasing remarks about the honeymoon being over, she had come by a couple of times on neighborly errands. Although she had been friendly enough, there was something about the woman's outspoken, forthright manner that made Amy uncomfortable around her.

Clad in a denim blouse and matching gathered skirt, Francine looked stylish and chic, as usual. She seemed to be caught off guard as she took in Amy's attire. She recovered her poise quickly, though. "Why, Amy, don't you look—sweet." Somehow, she made it sound like a put-down.

Summoning a smile, Amy murmured a brief "Thank you." She shot Reese a look that clearly said, *What's she doing here?*

"Oh, I guess I forgot to mention that Francine is riding over to the Kramers' with us," Reese explained.

"My car is in the shop, and Dad can't get to the dance until later," Francine put in. "I had one of the hands bring me over here so I can catch a ride with you and Reese. You don't mind, do you, dear?"

"No, of course not," Amy replied, resisting the urge to snap, *And don't call me dear.* Actually, she did mind, very much, although she couldn't say exactly why.

Chapter Thirteen

Colored lanterns were strung about the Kramers' barn, giving it a festive look. The smell of new wood mingled with the scent of hay and the tangy aroma of barbecuing meat. The twang of country-western music filled the air.

Reese barely noticed any of this, though. He was just relieved that the ride to the barn dance was over. He felt as worn out as if he'd been fighting wildcats.

Although the cab of his pickup truck was easily roomy enough to accommodate himself and two passengers, it had seemed stuffy and crowded. He supposed it was because of the not-so-subtle undercurrents and nuances floating around.

He'd sensed a certain tension between Amy and Francine—he'd have to be blind not to see it—and he had a fairly good idea what was behind it. He was aware that Francine had always considered them to be a couple. To his knowledge, he'd done nothing to encourage her. He'd been too busy running his ranch to really work at developing a relationship—with her or any of the unattached women of his acquaintance. True, he and Francine had occasionally attended local social functions together, but that was primarily because they were close neighbors, and sometimes it was simply more convenient to go someplace together than to take separate vehicles.

Besides, she wasn't his type. He wasn't sure exactly what his type was, but he was reasonably sure Francine wasn't it. The image that flashed across his mind when he tried to picture his "type" was of someone very much like Amy. It was a disquieting thought.

As the trio entered the barn, he noticed more than one glance of male appreciation directed toward Amy. Haley greeted her with a quick hug around the waist and a "Wow! You look terrific."

Herb and Iris detached themselves from a group of guests and made their way through the couples on the makeshift dance floor to come over and welcome them. "Ah, the newlyweds," Iris said, beaming at them benevolently. "And . . ." Her brow furrowed slightly as her gaze shifted to Francine, on Reese's other side.

"I begged a ride with Reese and Amy," Francine explained with a smile. "Dad can't get here until later, and I didn't want to miss out on the fun. Reese and I always enjoy your parties so much, don't we?" She turned to Reese for verification.

He wasn't quite sure how to respond to her remark. Francine's manner implied a closeness between them that existed only in her imagination.

Herb's jovial "Glad you could make it" eased them past the slightly uncomfortable moment. "Barbecue's almost ready. Get yourself something to drink in the meantime." He nodded in the direction of the refreshment table.

As the Kramers' attention was claimed by another of their guests, Francine exclaimed, "Oh, that song they're playing is a favorite of mine." She turned to Reese. "Dance with me, please."

The last thing Reese wanted to do was dance with Francine. He wasn't much for dancing in the first place, but if he had to do so, he wanted it to be with Amy. Ever since he'd seen her coming down the stairs tonight in that blue dress, he'd been thinking about how the bodice clung to her slender curves, and how the full skirt swirled around her slim legs.

He wanted to hold her close, to feel her softness pressed against his body. . . .

He was about to make some excuse to Francine, but before he could utter a word she linked her arm through his and drew him toward the dance floor.

All at once Amy was overcome by a flash of anger so strong it took her by surprise. Who did Francine think she was, anyway? Marriage of convenience or not, Reese was *her* husband, and she had no intention of standing idly by while another woman made a play for him. Besides, she reminded herself, there were a lot of people watching. It was important that they keep up the charade of being loving newlyweds.

With a determination she hadn't realized she possessed, she marched onto the dance floor just as Francine was turning to face Reese. Deftly, she stepped between them. Glancing over her shoulder at Francine, she smiled her sweetest smile. "I'd like to dance with my husband. I'm sure you won't mind."

It wasn't until she reached up to put her hand on Reese's shoulder that she began to regret her impulsive action. Maybe he *wanted* to dance with Francine. But when he took her in his arms, the sensations generated by his nearness drove all thoughts of Francine from her mind. The music that was playing was a slow, sensuous love song, and he pulled her close, so that her head was nestled in the hollow just below his shoulder. She inhaled deeply. The tangy scent of some kind of masculine aftershave mingled with the smell of leather and the outdoors. She'd never realized before what a heady combination that could be.

As they swayed together in time to the soft, liquid music, she felt a tingling sensation every place his body touched hers, as if little currents of electricity were running through her.

When the number was over Reese seemed reluctant to release her. Or did she just imagine that? "Let's go get something cold to drink," he suggested, taking her hand. As he escorted her to the refreshment table he said, "By the way, thanks for rescuing me out there."

"I, ah, wasn't sure you wanted to be rescued."

"Believe me, I did," he assured her with a wry smile. Amy was surprised at how relieved she was to hear him say so. "Francine and I have known each other for years," he went on, "but I think she reads a whole lot into our relationship that doesn't exist." There was a note of earnestness in his voice, as if it was important that Amy understand there was nothing between him and Francine. "I'm sorry if she's been giving you a hard time. . . ." His words trailed off, and he muttered a low "Oh, no" under his breath. Following his glance, Amy saw Francine heading in their direction.

Just before she reached them she was intercepted by Jake. "Howdy, Miz Hammond," he said gallantly. "I'd be mighty pleased if I could have this next dance."

"Oh, ah . . ." Francine's usual poise apparently deserted her as a variety of emotions played across her features. She seemed to be struggling to hide her dismay. But before she could find the right words to politely decline, Jake swept her onto the dance floor. This time the music had a lively, foot-stomping beat, and Jake threw himself into it with enthusiasm, vigorously whirling his obviously reluctant partner around the floor.

Bless Jake, Amy thought. She knew the crusty old cowboy had no great affection for Francine, that he had only asked her to dance to keep her occupied.

As she and Reese stood on the sidelines, she spotted Haley and Will on the dance floor. They had apparently noticed the little scene that had just taken place. Haley grinned, gesturing in Francine's direction with her chin, and Will gave them an approving thumbs-up as they danced past.

When the music came to an end, Amy saw Francine ease out of Jake's embrace. Jake said something to her, and, with a smile that looked a little strained, Francine shook her head. Tucking her shirt back into the waistband of her gathered skirt and attempting, somewhat ineffectually, to pat her disheveled hair back into place, she glanced around as if she were looking for someone.

It was time, Amy decided, to make it clear to Francine that Reese was *her* husband—and he wasn't up for grabs.

Moving closer to Reese, she put a hand on his arm in a patently possessive gesture. At her touch, Reese looked down at her in mild surprise. She held her breath, wondering if she was being too . . . she wasn't sure what. Clingy? Apparently, Reese didn't think so, though, as he put his own hand over hers.

That gave her the encouragement she needed. She concentrated all her energy on demonstrating to Francine—or anyone else who happened to be watching—what a devoted couple she and Reese were.

She glanced up at him through lowered lashes, as if they had some intimate secret between them. She hung on his every word with rapt attention, and when he made a witty remark, she favored him with her most radiant smile.

To his credit, Reese played his own part well. Oh, at first he'd seemed somewhat puzzled, but then his expression had cleared, as if he realized what she was doing, and why. He stayed close to her side the entire evening, as if he couldn't bear to be separated from her for even a few moments. Occasionally, he put an arm around her waist in a casually affectionate way. And when they danced together—only to the slow numbers—he held her tenderly, as if she were fragile and delicate.

Somewhere along the way, Amy began to sense a subtle change, an invisible *something* building up between them. Maybe it was because of the expression in his eyes when he looked down at her, or the way his very touch made her feel all warm inside—as if her bones were melting—but all at once she had the disquieting feeling they were no longer playacting.

Had she gone too far? she wondered. A little voice in the back of her mind warned her that maybe it was time to put some distance between herself and Reese, before the situation got out of hand. She brushed it aside. Enveloped in this rosy glow, she found it easy to convince herself Reese was just playing his part convincingly.

Taking her hand, he led her over to a shadowy, relatively private corner of the barn. Once they were away from prying eyes and curious glances, he put his hands on her shoulders and gently turned her so that she was facing him. *It's now or never,* she thought. She had to put a stop to this— while she was still able to think rationally. . . .

"Reese" she began, "maybe we shouldn't—" But her words died on her lips as she looked into his eyes.

She realized, even before he took her in his arms, that he was going to kiss her. She knew she should pull away, go back to where there were lights, and people, but she couldn't seem to make her limbs obey her will. She felt mesmerized, unable to move when Reese's lips brushed across hers.

At first his kiss was light, almost cautious, as if he were venturing into uncharted territory and wasn't sure what to expect. In spite of his hesitancy, though, something exploded in the pit of Amy's stomach the second his lips touched hers. She felt, rather than heard, his sudden intake of breath as he sensed the response she wasn't able to hide. Then all traces of uncertainty vanished and the pressure of his mouth increased until her lips softened under his.

When they pulled apart he drew a deep, ragged breath. "Why don't we get out of here?" he whispered.

Even though her every instinct warned her she was playing with fire, she found herself nodding her assent.

After a quick glance around to make sure they weren't being observed, they slipped out one of the side doors. When Reese put his hand under her elbow to guide her across the darkened lawn, the light touch sent a tingle all the way up her arm.

Once they were in the truck, Amy found herself suddenly nervous. What had she gotten herself into? She slid all the way over by the passenger door, in a kind of instinctively protective move. Reese glanced over at her, a question in his eyes. Then he wrapped an arm around her and pulled her close to him. "That's better," he said, steering the truck with his left hand and keeping his right arm around her.

She could hear his heart pounding against her ear. Or was that her own heart?

When they arrived at the ranch, the house was dark except for a faint light burning in the kitchen. That meant Mattie and the children had retired for the night—and she and Reese would be alone. She realized she'd been subconsciously hoping the housekeeper would still be up.

She wondered if Reese could feel her trembling as they walked toward the house together. She couldn't imagine what had possessed her to let her guard down the way she had.

He held the door open, waiting for her to go in ahead of him. When she hesitated he gave her a questioning glance. All at once she felt a stab of panic. She couldn't just stand here on the porch, as if she'd suddenly turned to stone. As she edged past him, she couldn't help brushing against him. Despite her determination to maintain an outward calm, her body hummed in response to his closeness.

He followed her inside and pulled the door shut behind them. There was something dismayingly final about that little metallic click as it closed. The thought crossed her mind that it was the sound of her fate being sealed.

She told herself to stop being melodramatic. All she had to do, if she wanted to let him know he had completely misinterpreted her intentions, was to maintain a cool, reserved demeanor.

Once they were inside, she leaned back against the door as if it represented some kind of security or protection. She realized that hadn't been a wise move, though, when Reese turned to face her. She wished he wouldn't stand quite so close. It made it difficult to form any kind of coherent thought. She drew a deep breath. Where was she? Oh, yes—she was about to demonstrate *cool* and *reserved*.

Her good intentions disappeared like a puff of smoke, though, when he took her in his arms. The sensations generated by being held against that lean, muscular body were causing a sweetness to spread through her entire being, robbing her of any will to resist. When he lowered his head and his lips caressed hers, she returned his kisses with an eagerness that would have shocked her had she been able to think clearly.

They jerked apart as a shrill, high-pitched shriek cut through the stillness. It was coming from upstairs.

"Chrissie!" they both exclaimed in unison.

In seconds Reese was bounding up the stairs, two at a time, with Amy close behind. Her heart was pounding, and a million thoughts whirled through her mind. Was Chrissie sick? Was there an intruder?

She reached the little girl's room a few steps behind Reese, who flicked the light switch on as he dashed through the door. A few seconds later Mattie appeared in the doorway, pulling her robe around her.

Chrissie was sitting up in bed crying, her small body trembling. "What is it, sweetheart?" Reese asked, rushing to her bedside and taking her in his arms.

At first she only sobbed harder, burying her face against his shoulder. "There, there, it's all right," he murmured, patting her gently.

Gradually, she began to calm down. "There—there was a monster in my room." she said between sobs. "It was . . ." She paused to take a deep, shuddering breath. "It was a great big *scary* monster."

"A monster, huh?" Reese continued his soothing ministrations as he considered this. "I think you had a bad dream. Why don't I check and make sure there are no monsters."

"No!" Her small hands clutched at him as he started to get up.

He sat back down. "Aunt Amy's going to stay right here with you, while I look for monsters. Okay?"

After a few moments she loosened her grip on him. "O-okay," she said, wiping her eyes with the back of her hand.

Slowly, Reese eased himself up off the bed. Amy took his place, putting an arm around the child protectively. Reese thoroughly inspected the closet, under the bed, and even in the dresser drawers—which coaxed a reluctant giggle from Chrissie.

Mattie had been watching all this from the doorway. ''I'll go heat some milk for her,'' she said, apparently satisfied that Reese and Amy had the situation well in hand.

It was late by the time the room had been pronounced monster free and Chrissie had been soothed back to sleep with warm milk and a lot of comforting and reassurances. Amy felt completely drained. Any last, lingering traces of the sudden, unexpected electricity that had sprung up between her and Reese had long since dissipated—at least on her part. A glance at Reese's drawn features told her he felt the same way.

As she tucked the blanket around the sleeping child and tiptoed out of the room, she couldn't help wondering what would have happened if fate hadn't stepped in, in the form of Chrissie's bad dream.

Chapter Fourteen

Amy lay awake far into the night, reliving the events of the evening. She could hardly believe she'd let down her guard that way. She was appalled at how close she had come to violating the "strictly business" agreement between herself and Reese.

By the next morning she knew what had to be done. It was time to put an end to this sham marriage. It had accomplished its purpose. He had what he wanted—custody of the children. She'd fulfilled her part of the bargain, and there was no reason for her to stick around any longer. The wisest thing she could do would be to get out now—before she lost what little self-control she had left.

Although the thought of saying good-bye to Kevin and Chrissie, Mattie, the friends she'd made here, and—yes—Reese too, left her feeling empty inside, she didn't see what other choice she had. She couldn't possibly continue living in the same house with Reese, not when she knew the effect he had on her.

The plan had sounded so simple in theory—a quick marriage, an even quicker divorce or annulment, once their purpose had been accomplished. She hadn't anticipated falling in love with the little town of Red Deer and the

145

surrounding area, with its warm, friendly inhabitants, though.

She also hadn't anticipated falling in love with Reese. For she'd had to admit, as she lay staring into the darkness last night, that she was hopelessly, irrevocably in love with him.

She didn't dare let him know, of course. That would only make matters worse. She would simply explain to him, clearly and unemotionally, that she'd decided it was time for her to leave, to get on with her life. Although he might offer a token protest or two, he would likely be vastly relieved. Probably, he was as appalled as she was over how far things had gone last night.

She didn't have to go back to Seattle. She had no ties there now. She wasn't sure just where she would go. Reese had suggested, when he'd first approached her with this plan, that she might want to consider making her home in Red Deer or one of the neighboring towns, so she could be near the children. She knew she couldn't bear the thought of being so close to Reese and having to hide her feelings, though. Besides, it would be embarrassing to face the friends she'd made here, knowing they would all be wondering what had happened between her and Reese.

No, she'd be better off to go someplace where nobody knew her, where she could make a brand-new start.

At least she wouldn't have to worry about whether Chrissie and Kevin would be properly cared for after she left. Between Reese and Mattie, they would be much better off than if she had tried to raise them herself. Already they were so content in their new home that she was sure they would barely notice she was gone after the first few days.

That thought failed to make her feel any better.

Telling Mattie she was leaving wasn't going to be easy

either. She was going to miss the plainspoken, good-hearted woman.

But the first order of business was to let Reese know of her decision. She planned her little speech carefully, going over it several times in her mind. As soon as she had a chance to talk to him in private, she'd tell him of her plans. That done, she could be on her way in a day or two. Now that she'd made up her mind, there was no point in prolonging things.

When Reese came in around midmorning and poured himself a cup of coffee, Amy took a deep breath, steeling herself for the confrontation. Usually, he drank his coffee in the kitchen, leaning casually against the counter. This morning, though, he took his cup and, with a brief nod to Amy, headed for the small room just off the living room that served as his office.

She wondered if he was deliberately avoiding her. It occurred to her that he might be afraid she'd read more into his behavior last night than he'd intended. If that was the case, he needn't worry, she told herself. She wouldn't dream of presuming on what she was sure had been nothing more than a momentary lapse of good judgment on his part.

He had left the door slightly ajar, and she pushed it open and slipped into the office, closing it behind her. He was just starting to sit down at his desk, and he glanced up at her in mild surprise.

''I—I need to discuss something with you,'' she said.

An expression of wariness came over his features. So she'd been right, she thought. He *was* worried. What did he think she was going to do, for Pete's sake, throw herself into his arms? She'd better get this over with as soon as possible, she decided, to put his mind at rest.

All at once however, she couldn't seem to remember a word of her carefully prepared little speech.

Reese cleared his throat nervously. "Ah, Amy, about last night . . ."

It was the *about last night* that jolted her out of her temporary attack of speechlessness. The last thing she wanted to hear was Reese explaining to her, apologetically, that last night had been a mistake, that he was sorry he'd allowed the situation to get out of hand, and she could rest assured it wouldn't happen again.

"Reese, I'm going away," she blurted out.

"Going away?" He frowned. "What do you mean? Going where?"

She clasped her hands together to keep them from trembling. "We've stayed married long enough to accomplish what we set out to do. I think we can safely end it now."

He seemed to be having trouble taking this in. "Have you thought this out? There's no need to rush into anything."

"I'm not rushing into it. I *have* given it a lot of thought."

He got up and came around the desk. She wished he wouldn't stand quite so close. It made it hard for her to stick to her resolve.

"You're welcome to stay as long as you like, you know."

"I can't just go on indefinitely, being a . . . a prop in this little charade we've been acting out. It's time for me to start getting on with my life." She didn't dare let him know she'd like nothing better than to stay here the rest of her life, that this ranch, in the short time she'd been here, had come to mean *home* to her, that the friends she'd made here were like family.

Or that she'd gladly go on being his wife.

She hoped at least to leave with her few remaining shreds of pride intact.

"What about the kids?" Reese asked.

"What about them? It isn't as if I'm abandoning them. You were the one who convinced me they'll be better off with you. You know that's the only reason I agreed to this plan in the first place. I'll come back to see them as often as I can, of course, but they're already so settled here I doubt if they'll even realize I'm gone—" She broke off. She didn't want him to know she was having trouble speaking around the lump in her throat.

There was an expression on his features she didn't understand. Was it pity? She shrank from the thought of having him feel sorry for her.

He reached out as if to put his hands on her shoulders, then apparently thought better of it. He dropped his hands to his sides.

She hoped her sigh of relief wasn't too noticeable. If he so much as touched her she was afraid she'd completely lose her already tenuous hold on her self-control and end up sobbing against his chest. Why couldn't he have made this easy for both of them by simply accepting the fact that she was leaving?

"You're not going anyplace right now, are you?" he asked. "I mean, not for a couple of weeks, anyway?"

"I, ah, expect to be on my way by tomorrow, or the next day, at the latest." She was surprised at how calm her voice sounded. Nobody would be able to tell, from listening to her, that her heart was breaking.

"So soon?" The lines in Reese's face deepened. "Can't we talk this over?"

"There's nothing to talk about," she said firmly. "We both knew this was just a temporary arrangement." With that, she turned and left the room.

Reese stared after her, openmouthed.

What had gotten into her? And what had she meant about

getting on with her life? Was there some guy waiting in the wings for her when she'd fulfilled her commitment to help him obtain custody of the kids? Although she'd never mentioned a man in her life, he supposed it was unrealistic of him to think she didn't have a serious boyfriend or two back in Seattle. She was young and attractive. He wondered why it had never occurred to him that she probably had guys swarming around her like bees around honey.

He slumped into the chair behind his desk, but the paperwork he'd come in to take care of was completely forgotten. After a few minutes he jammed his hat on his head and stomped out of the room.

"Something wrong, boss?"

Reese and Curly were on the roof of the barn, repairing the damage done by the last windstorm. "What makes you think there's anything wrong?" Reese asked, not looking up from his work.

Curly scratched his chin. "Well, it sure ain't because of your sparkling personality."

Reese glared at him. "What's that supposed to mean?"

"Oh, nothing," Curly replied innocently. "It's just that you don't seem to be in a real good mood today."

"Sorry," Reese snapped. "I didn't realize I was supposed to be a ray of sunshine."

"Hey, I didn't mean to get you riled up," Curly said, with an air of offended dignity. "There ain't no denying, though, you seem a mite testy today."

Reese turned his attention back to the task at hand. His only comment was a muffled, "Hmph." Although wild horses couldn't have dragged the admission out of him, he knew he *was* being—as Curly put it—"a mite testy."

He was fully aware, of course, of the reason for his less than pleasant mood. Amy's unexpected announcement had knocked him for a loop. He'd thought everything was going along smoothly. The kids were happy and well adjusted. Amy was fitting nicely into ranch life. Why would she want to just up and leave?

He supposed she was upset over what had happened last night. He knew he'd overstepped his bounds. In fact, he'd been about to offer her an apology, to reassure her that it had been a momentary lapse and it would never happen again, when she'd dropped her little bombshell.

He'd known, of course, that they'd eventually go their separate ways. He just hadn't expected it to be so soon.

He tried to imagine what it would be like around here without Amy. He'd become accustomed to seeing her when he came up to the house for a break, helping Mattie in the kitchen, or maybe playing with the kids. He'd enjoyed the times she'd accompanied him as he went about his ranch chores.

He muttered something unintelligible under his breath. Why did she want to go and mess up everything?

Other than a slight lifting of his eyebrows, Curly gave no indication that he'd noticed the brief outburst. "Would you pass them nails over?" he asked.

"Huh?" Reese blinked uncomprehendingly, as if his hired hand had said something in another language.

"Nails," Curly prompted.

"Oh." Reese slid the can of nails to him.

They worked in silence for several minutes. Reese tried to shut out the images that kept flitting across his consciousness—of Amy admiring an unusual rock, or even a worm that Kevin had brought in to show her; Amy reading a bedtime story to Chrissie; Amy in that blue dress that clung to her figure—

"Ouch!" He dropped his hammer and grasped the thumb he had just pounded.

"Maybe you better let me finish this," Curly suggested mildly. "It ain't a real good idea for someone whose mind ain't on his work to be up on a roof."

Without bothering to reply, Reese made his way over to the ladder and climbed down, being careful not to further injure his throbbing thumb.

With the air of a man who had just come to a decision, he strode across the yard and into the house. Mattie, sitting in the rocking chair with a basket of mending on the floor beside her, looked up from her sewing in surprise as he burst into the den. His brief "Where's Amy?" effectively discouraged any comments about his demeanor, however.

"I think she's up in her room."

He marched up the stairs and pounded on Amy's door.

"What on earth . . ." she began, opening the door. Her words trailed off as she saw Reese's expression.

"We need to talk," Reese said. "You walked off before we finished our conversation this morning."

"There wasn't anything left to say." She started to close the door, but Reese put a hand on it.

"There's a whole lot to say." He paused, taking a deep breath to calm himself. He knew it wouldn't help his cause any to force his way into her room. "Can I come in?"

Amy started to protest; then, as if she realized he wasn't going to be deterred, she opened the door wider to admit him.

Once he was inside he wasn't sure just what he was going to say to her. He'd intended to try to talk some sense into her, but he was distracted by the sight of her open suitcase on the bed, partially packed.

"You're really serious about this, then?"

"Of course I am," she replied, looking surprised.

"I really think you should give this more thought. We could discuss it."

She sighed. ''We've already been through this. There's nothing to think over, nothing to discuss.''

''Amy, listen—if you're leaving because of last night, you have my promise it'll never happen—''

His words were interrupted by a light tap at the door, accompanied by Mattie's, ''Could both of you come out here?''

''We're, ah, kind of busy right now,'' Reese replied. ''Can it wait?''

After a pause, Mattie said, ''Not really. You have a visitor.''

''Whoever it is, could you handle things?''

''I really think this is something you should take care of yourself.'' There was a note in Mattie's voice that couldn't be ignored.

''We'd better go see what this is all about,'' Reese said to Amy. ''We'll have to finish this discussion later.''

''It's already finished,'' she answered quietly. ''I told you, there's nothing left to discuss.''

He opened the door and stepped aside so she could go out ahead of him. ''Please don't do anything until we've had time for a long talk.''

Amy wanted to have this over and done with. Apparently, though, it was going to have to wait until they dealt with this visitor. With a helpless shrug, she edged past him, being careful to not brush against him. She was aware of the effect the slightest contact could have on her, how little it would take for her resolve to vanish like a puff of smoke.

She felt self-conscious as she made her way down the stairs. She was aware of his gaze on her.

''Amy, my dear, how wonderful to see you again.''

A shock wave ran through her as Stanly Bender stepped up to greet her.

Chapter Fifteen

Taken completely by surprise, Amy wasn't quick enough to elude Stanly when he took her hand in his. She did manage to duck back out of the way, though, when he attempted to kiss her cheek.

He glanced down at her with a concern that was obviously false. "You look pale, my dear. Are you all right?"

Stifling the urge to snap, *I was until you showed up,* she pulled her hand away. Reese was looking at her in a way that clearly said, *What's he doing here?*

She lifted one shoulder in a brief shrug to indicate she was as much in the dark as he was.

"I had to come out this way on a business trip. . . ." Stanly began.

Amy eyed him suspiciously. The only "business" she'd ever known Stanly to be involved in was monkey business.

"So I decided this would be a good opportunity to drop by and see how Kenny and Chrissie are doing—"

"Kevin," Amy corrected dryly.

"I beg your pardon?"

"It's Kevin. His name is Kevin—not Kenny."

"Of course. Kevin." Stanly cleared his throat. "I think the world of those children, you know," he went on, undaunted, ''and I'm naturally concerned for their well-being.''

Sure. Amy thought. It was their money he thought the world of. She knew he was only here to snoop around. He was still hoping to find some grounds for challenging the court's custody decision. If he could come up with any reason to suspect there was anything out of the ordinary about her marriage to Reese, he would redouble his efforts to gain custody of Kevin and Chrissie.

''I rented a car at the airport in Laramie and drove right out here,'' Stanly explained, ''so I could see those children.''

''The kids are fine,'' Reese said in clipped tones.

Stanly's patently false smile slipped just a bit at the coldness in Reese's voice, but he quickly recovered his equilibrium. ''I must say, I expected a warmer welcome. That housekeeper of yours made me feel as if I were some kind of intruder, even after I explained to her that I'm Amy's uncle. You really should train your hired help to treat visitors with the proper respect.''

Amy glanced over at Mattie, who was standing off to one side. Although her face was an impassive mask, everything else about her exuded anger and disapproval.

''Mattie isn't hired help,'' Reese snapped. ''She's part of the family.''

Amy noticed the icy look in Reese's eyes, and the way the muscle in his jaw twitched, as if his teeth were tightly clenched. He looked as if he were on the verge of tossing the unwelcome visitor out on his ear. As satisfying as she would have found that, she knew that antagonizing Stanly would be a tactical error. She and Reese still had the upper hand as long as they could keep him from knowing they were onto his game.

That meant, of course, keeping up their charade for a while longer. The idea filled her with dismay. She simply wanted to be free of the whole complicated mess, to go away someplace where she could begin putting Reese out of her mind, so she could—eventually—start leading a normal life—or at least try to.

But the important thing, for the moment, was to make sure Stanly left with absolutely no doubts about the genuineness of their marriage. And the sooner he was convinced, the sooner he'd be on his way.

Moving closer to Reese, she smiled up at him with what she hoped was a look of rapt adoration. "Darling," she said, "I'm sure Stanly must be tired after his long trip. Why don't we have Mattie show him to his room?" She knew this wouldn't sit too well with Mattie, but she'd have to smooth things over later.

The lines in Reese's face deepened, and a frown creased his brow. Amy's glance caught his, sending a silent signal: *Just play along.*

"Would you like me to make up a room for Mr. Bender?" Mattie asked, her voice expressionless.

Amy tried to cover her surprise. A few moments ago Mattie had looked ready to do battle. Now she was a model of the perfect servant, humble and subservient, her only wish to do her employer's bidding.

"I think maybe the south bedroom," the housekeeper suggested.

Of course. Mattie had explained to her, when she first came here, about the south bedroom and why it was the least desirable room in the house. It was situated in such a way that in summer it caught the full force of the sun, so that by midafternoon it was like an oven. Conversely, during the winter months it was always cold and drafty. The branches of a huge oak tree draped over that corner of the house, dropping acorns and attracting squirrels. The room had become a receptacle for old, cast-off furniture, including a mattress so worn and lumpy that getting a decent night's sleep on it was practically an impossibility.

Amy smiled. "The south bedroom would be perfect."

"I'm afraid you'll have to see to our guest," Reese said. "I, ah, was right in the middle of something."

Coward, Amy thought.

Reese started to leave, then turned back. Taking Amy in his arms, he brushed his lips across hers in a kiss that, even though she was aware that he was only putting on a show for Stanly's benefit, set all her senses tingling. "I'll see you at dinnertime," he murmured, somehow managing to convey the impression, to anyone who happened to be observing, that he would be counting the minutes.

With that, he made a hasty exit, leaving her to deal with Stanly. "I'm sure you'd like to freshen up before dinner," she said with a cordiality she didn't feel. "Mattie will show you to your room."

As he turned to follow Mattie up the stairs, Amy caught a glimpse of movement out of the corner of her eye. Chrissie and Kevin, ever curious, had come running in from another part of the house to see who the company was. They came to a sudden halt in the doorway when they saw Stanly. Taking only a second or two to size up the situation, Kevin grabbed his sister's hand and yanked her back out of sight before Stanly spotted them.

Dinner was an uncomfortable affair. Usually the evening meal was eaten family style, with Amy, Reese, Mattie, and the children all gathered together around the table. Tonight, though, Mattie declined to join them, and Amy sensed she was still smarting over Stanly's remark about "hired help." She served the food in tight-lipped silence.

Only Stanly seemed unaware of the tension around the table. "How're you youngsters doing?" he asked Kevin and Chrissie in an overly hearty tone. "My wife Irene and I have really missed you. For a while there, before your Aunt Amy and Uncle Reese got married, we were hoping you'd come and live with us."

This bit of information caused the children to exchange alarmed looks.

Stanly appeared not to notice. "Tell me all about what it's like living here with Aunt Amy and Uncle Reese," he coaxed.

He was trying to pump them for any information he could use for his own benefit, Amy realized. His attempts met with little success, however. Kevin, eyeing him with suspicion, replied in almost sullen monosyllables, and Chrissie fell back into her old habit of retreating behind a wall of shyness.

When Stanly's attention was diverted briefly by Reese asking him to pass the potatoes, Amy felt a slight tug on her sleeve. As she glanced down at Kevin, he leaned close to her and whispered, "I don't like that man."

She mouthed the words, "Neither do I."

The minute dinner was over Reese disappeared again with a vague alibi about something important that needed his attention.

Once Stanly was settled in the living room with an after-dinner cup of coffee, Amy excused herself, saying she was going to help Mattie with the cleaning up.

He frowned disapprovingly. "Isn't that what you pay that woman for? You need to learn to be firm with these people, or they'll walk all over you."

Amy bit back the angry retort that sprang to her lips. With a murmured, "I'll be back in a little while," she made her exit before she was tempted to say anything she might regret.

In the kitchen she found Mattie grim and angry. ''How long is that awful man going to be here?'' she asked between clenched teeth.

''Not long, I hope,'' Amy replied with a heartfelt sigh as she helped load the dishwasher. ''I'd like to tell him to hit the road, but you know how important it is to convince him that Reese and I are happily married. If he thinks there's anything the least bit out of order, he'll use it to try to get custody of the children.''

''He'd better not even *think* of trying to take those babies away from here, if he knows what's good for him,'' Mattie threatened darkly.

When Amy was finished in the kitchen she was tempted to find some other household chores to keep her occupied so she wouldn't have to spend her evening entertaining Stanly. She decided it wouldn't be a good idea to leave him by himself for any length of time, though. If she didn't keep a close watch on him, he was likely to go snooping around on his own, just to see if he could find out anything that might be of use to him.

She had no doubt her suspicions were confirmed when she returned to the living room and found him looking at the desk in the corner. She could have sworn she'd heard the distinctive sound of the rolltop being closed, just before she entered the room. ''I was just admiring this desk,'' he said, running a hand over the polished wood. ''They don't make furniture like this these days.''

''It's been in Reese's family for a long time,'' she said, struggling to keep her anger from showing. She would have been willing to bet he'd been poking through the contents of the desk. Fortunately, there was nothing in it of a personal nature.

Unperturbed at having been almost caught in the act of snooping through someone else's possessions, Stanly casually strolled back to where he had been sitting, and picked up his coffee cup.

Time seemed to grind to a halt as Amy struggled to make polite conversation with him. She felt a flash of resentment at Reese for having made his escape, leaving her to deal with their guest.

When Reese finally came in from wherever he'd been hiding out, he stopped dead still in the doorway, his expression mirroring his dismay. "Still up, I see. I thought you'd be worn out from your trip, and would want to turn in early."

Before he could retreat, Amy jumped up quickly. "I'd better start getting Kevin and Chrissie ready for bed." As she passed Reese in the doorway she stood on tiptoe and raised her face to his so that, to anyone watching from behind, it would appear that she was kissing him. Instead, she whispered in his ear, "Keep an eye on him. He's tricky."

She drew out the supervision of baths and bedtime as long as she could. Eventually, though, the children were tucked into their beds, and she had no excuse for not returning to the living room. She found Reese silent and uncommunicative, responding to Stanly's attempts at small talk only when it was absolutely necessary, and then in terse, clipped tones. For the next twenty minutes or so, conversation limped along. Reese made no effort to hide his yawns, and several times he glanced at his watch pointedly.

After what seemed an eternity, Stanly stood up and stretched. "I hate to break up such a pleasant evening," he said, "but I am a little tired. I think I'll turn in."

*   *   *

Amy's first instinct, upon awakening the next morning, was just to pull the covers over her head and stay in bed all day, so she wouldn't have to deal with Stanly. She knew that ignoring the problem wouldn't make it go away, though. Left unsupervised, Stanly could have the whole place in an uproar. Reluctantly, she pushed the blanket aside and got out of bed.

When she went downstairs, Reese was nowhere to be seen. He'd likely been up for hours, and had found some kind of chore that would keep him out on the range most of the day—where he wouldn't have to encounter Stanly.

She found Mattie in the kitchen, fuming. "He had the nerve to criticize my cooking," the housekeeper muttered, wiping off an already spotless counter. She wielded the dishcloth as if it were a weapon. "Said the biscuits were 'a little heavy.' I'll have him know my biscuits took a blue ribbon three years running at the county fair. Anyway, I noticed it didn't seem to hurt his appetite any."

She stopped wiping the counter and fixed Amy with a steady look. "If that man stays here another day I can't be responsible for what I might do," she threatened darkly.

"Mattie, I'm really sorry about this."

"I know it's not your fault," Mattie said. Then she brightened. "Maybe he'll leave soon. He was complaining about how badly he'd slept. Said the mattress was lumpy, and when he finally did get to sleep he was awakened when it was barely daylight by some kind of animals running around on the roof."

A conspiratorial smile passed between the two women, before Amy asked, "Do you know where he is now?"

"Said he was going outside to have a look around the ranch."

Amy sighed. "I suppose I'd better get out there and keep an eye on him."

* * *

Muttering under his breath, Reese attacked the tangle of brush, twigs, and other debris with a vengeance, as if they were his personal enemies.

He didn't have to be out here spending time unclogging water holes, of course. He had a whole crew of men to take care of that sort of thing, leaving him free to handle the administrative duties of running the ranch. The vigorous physical activity was just what he needed, though, to work off the restlessness that was building up inside him, making him feel like a volcano that was about to explode.

It wasn't just Stanly's arrival that had driven him out of the house. Amy's unexpected announcement yesterday that she was planning to leave in a day or two had completely knocked him for a loop.

He'd spent a restless night tossing and turning. It didn't help any that every time he started to doze, his dreams were haunted by the memory of the way her slender curves had pressed against the hard planes of his own body as they'd danced, the softness of her lips when he'd kissed her.

Finally, just as the first faint streaks of daylight were becoming visible, he'd given up trying to get any sleep. He'd gotten up before the rest of the household was stirring, tiptoeing around so he wouldn't awaken anyone. He wasn't in the mood for company or conversation just now.

After a hasty breakfast he'd loaded the Jeep with an assortment of tools and implements for whatever chore he could find to do, eased it out of the yard, and headed for the farthest corner of the ranch. He needed to put as much distance between himself and Amy as possible while he sorted out his feelings.

So here he was, out in a remote section of the ranch, hacking away at the debris clogging a water hole as if his life depended on it. A couple of heifers regarded him with mild curiosity, then turned and ambled away.

Gradually, as the vigorous exertion began to have the desired effect, he was able to regard the situation with some degree of rationality.

If Amy was determined to leave, he supposed it would simplify matters if he just kept still and let her go, instead of trying to change her mind. It wasn't fair to make her feel guilty about it. She had a right to get on with her life. Eventually she'd meet someone she cared about, and she'd want a real marriage, not this sham he'd talked her into.

He jabbed viciously at the pile of debris with his hoe. The thought of Amy being married to someone else was like a knife twisting inside him.

All at once, with no warning, the truth hit him. He was in love with her.

It was such a startling revelation that he ceased his attack on the water hole. Leaning on the handle of the hoe, he stared off into space as he tried to put this new knowledge into perspective. Falling in love had never been high on his list of priorities. He'd been too busy with other matters— running the ranch, looking after his younger sister Dina until she was grown, and, more recently, becoming guardian to Dina's kids. Yet, in spite of his vague conviction that there was no time in his schedule for romance, he had to admit he was head over heels in love with Amy.

It did no good to tell himself this was just a temporary infatuation, something he'd get over. Nor did he want to, he realized. There was no denying it—his life would be unbelievably barren and empty without her.

With that settled firmly in his mind, the next order of business was, *Where do we go from here?*

He supposed the next logical step would be to go to her, declare his love, and beg her to stay. Everything in him shrank from baring his heart and soul that way, though. What if she didn't love him in return?

He wasn't ever going to find out, though, by standing here shilly-shallying like a lovesick kid. Besides, he usually advocated a direct, "take the bull by the horns" approach to any situation.

With the air of a man with a purpose, he gathered up the hoe and other implements and tossed them into the back of the Jeep. Once he was face-to-face with Amy maybe he could get some idea of what her reaction would be to a declaration of love, and take things from there.

Chapter Sixteen

As Amy stepped outside, Kevin and Chrissie came running around the corner of the house and fell into step beside her. Chrissie slipped her hand into Amy's, and Kevin asked, "Where are you going, Aunt Amy? Can we go too?"

"I'm looking for Stanly. Have you seen him?"

At the mention of Stanly, the little boy made a face. "He's in the barn."

Chrissie immediately pulled her hand away. "I don't want to go. I don't like that man. He keeps asking if we want to come and live with him. We don't have to, do we?"

"No, honey, of course not."

"Good," Kevin said. "I'll be glad when he goes away." With that, both children ran back around to the side yard, where Reese had rigged up a tire swing for them.

Amy couldn't help thinking she too would be glad when Stanly went away.

She found him in the barn with Jake and Curly. He was attired in jeans so new they were still stiff, and Western boots, and he looked decidedly uncomfortable.

She had no doubt, from the little undercurrents of tension in the air, that he was being his usual less-than-charming self. Jake's jaw was tightly clenched, and even Curly's normally laid-back good nature seemed a little strained.

"I see you've, ah, met Stanly," she said.

"Yes, ma'am." Jake's tone revealed nothing of what he was thinking. "He told us to saddle up a horse for him so he could go for a ride and look the place over."

Amy didn't miss the slight emphasis on the "he told us." How like Stanly to demand, rather than ask, as if he had every right to order the ranch employees around.

"If it's all right with you, ma'am, we'll go out to the corral and pick out a horse for him," Jake went on, subtly making the point that he and Curly would be glad to take their orders from her, but not from Stanly.

"Why, ah, I suppose it's all right," Amy replied. If Stanly was out riding, at least that would keep him out of everyone's hair for a while.

Walking a little way behind as Curly ushered Stanly out of the barn, she noticed that Stanly was walking rather stiffly, and now and then he reached behind him to massage the small of his back.

"Did you sleep well, Stanly?" she asked sweetly.

He turned to look back at her. "Actually, no," he replied, scowling. "I had a miserable night. The mattress was lumpy, and when I finally did get to sleep a bunch of squirrels woke me up. They sounded like a herd of elephants running across the roof."

Jake fell into step beside Amy. She could tell by his manner he had something on his mind. Once Stanly was out of hearing range, he said, "Miz Cavanaugh, I don't like to say anything against somebody who's comp'ny here, but—well, this here Stanly's been giving everybody a hard time, throwing his weight around and criticizing the way we do our jobs. Besides that, he's been asking a lot of questions about things that really don't seem like any of his business, like how big the ranch is and how many head of cattle we've got.''

Jake's words caused a sinking feeling in the pit of Amy's stomach. She knew Stanly's sudden interest in ranching was more than idle curiosity. Knowing Stanly as she did, she was sure his next move would be to see if there was any way he could still gain something for himself.

''Begging your pardon, ma'am''—Jake's words interrupted her thoughts—''but he's making it awful hard for us to be polite to him.''

Oh, dear, Amy thought with dismay. If Stanly stayed around much longer he was going to cause a mutiny. Maybe it would be better to just let the hands know—at least the ones who had been in Reese's employ for a long time and could be depended on to keep it quiet—that Stanly's presence here was unasked-for and unwelcome, and they were under no obligation to put up with his rudeness.

Before she could figure out exactly how to word this, Curly stuck his head in the door. ''Hey, you two coming?''

''We'll be right there,'' she replied, hurrying to catch up.

When they reached the corral, Stanly was leaning his arms on the top railing, looking over the selection of horses. ''This here's a nice gentle one,'' Curly said, pointing out a mild-appearing mare.

Stanly gave him a withering look. ''I want a horse with some spirit, not some lead-footed nag that can't even stay awake. How about that one?''

Amy's glance followed Stanly's as he pointed out a buckskin on the other side of the corral.

Jake cleared his throat. ''I don't think you want to ride Pete. He needs a firm hand—''

"Are you questioning my riding ability?" Stanly shot back.

"No, sir, but there's something you ought to know about this horse."

As Amy listened to this exchange, bits and pieces of an earlier conversation she'd had with Jake came back to her. What had he said? "He don't like being ridden by someone who ain't had much experience . . . takes them under a tree with low-hanging branches . . . or . . . runs them up against a bush . . . brushes them right out of the saddle. . . ."

"Jake," Amy said quietly, "if Stanly wants to ride Pete, why don't we let him?"

Jake gave her a questioning look. "But Miz Cavanaugh . . ." His protests trailed off as Amy's glance caught his. "Whatever you say, ma'am," he replied.

As Jake and Curly saddled Pete, Jake explained to Stanly, "You gotta let him know who's boss."

"Yes, yes," Stanly said impatiently, "I know how to handle a horse."

When Pete was ready, Stanly swung into the saddle, reined the animal around, and nudged him into a trot. As Amy, Jake, and Curly watched him ride off, Jake shook his head. "Pete ain't gonna like the way he's sawing on them reins."

Curly glanced at his watch. "I'll give him fifteen minutes, at the most."

"Ten," Jake countered.

It took less time than that for Pete to come sauntering back—riderless, the reins trailing on the ground. "Now what have you gone and done?" Jake asked as the horse approached. Unrepentant, Pete stretched his neck forward and nuzzled Jake's shoulder.

When there was no sign of Stanly, Amy asked, "Do you think we should go out and look for him, or something?"

"I don't think that'll be necessary," Jake drawled. "It ain't likely he's hurt. Like I told you before, I've never known Pete to throw nobody."

"He don't need to," Curly put in. "He's got his own ways of getting rid of a rider."

When Amy spotted Stanly limping toward the barn, there was no mistaking his state of mind, even from a distance. Anger fairly radiated from him. As he drew nearer, it was obvious the most serious damage was to his dignity. There were a few minor scratches on his face and arms, as well as grass stains and smudges of dirt. His shirt pocket was torn, and a twig was entangled in his hair. Its leaves hung down over one eye, bobbing up and down with each step he took. He brushed at them ineffectually.

"Stanly, what happened?" Amy asked, striving to interject a note of concern into her voice.

"That *brute*," he ground out between clenched teeth, "should be taken out and shot. The first thing he did was head for a tree with low branches. Took me right under it. Somebody might have warned me about that horse. I'd almost think those hands of yours did it on purpose. You ought to fire the lot of them."

Amy was tempted to point out that he had insisted on riding Pete, but she was afraid if she opened her mouth she'd burst out laughing.

"I hope you realize I could have been seriously injured. I don't know why you keep a dangerous animal like that around—" He broke off in the middle of his tirade to glance at her curiously.

Shoulders shaking, Amy managed to get out a strangled "Excuse me" before she turned and ran for the house.

As soon as she was inside she closed the door behind her, leaned back against it, and gave in to the giggles she'd been stifling. Stanly had looked so funny, standing there seething with anger, covered with dirt and grass stains, leaves dangling down over one eye.

Once her mirth was exhausted, she took several deep, calming breaths. Although having a good laugh at Stanly's expense had provided a welcome diversion, it still wasn't enough to counteract her present mood. She felt tense and edgy, and her head was starting to ache. She needed to be by herself for a while.

Even in the sanctuary of her room, though, she found herself too restless to relax. How had everything gotten into such a tangled mess? she wondered. Nothing seemed to be working out the way it was supposed to. One factor she hadn't counted on when she'd agreed to this plan of Reese's was that she was going to fall in love with him. Nor had she anticipated his unexpected objections to her announcement that she was leaving.

She might as well finish her packing, she decided, dragging her luggage out from under the bed where she had hastily stashed it yesterday. When they finally did get rid of Stanly she wanted to be ready to carry out her decision to leave, without further delay.

As she began taking things from the closet and putting them in her suitcase, she recalled that she'd left some laundry in the clothes drier. She made a mental note to go downstairs and retrieve it before Reese came back from wherever he was hiding out, so she wouldn't take a chance on encountering him.

She wasn't sure she wanted to leave the privacy of her room just now, though. There seemed to be quite a lot of activity going on in the house; footsteps treading up and down the stairs and the hallway, doors opening and closing. She decided to wait until things quieted down before venturing downstairs.

On one of her trips back and forth from her closet to the

suitcase on her bed, a movement outside the window caught her attention. Glancing out, she could see Stanly's rental car in the driveway. Stanly was walking toward it, carrying his suitcase. Curious, she took a step back so she could watch him without being seen.

After putting his suitcase in the trunk, he went around to the driver's side and opened the door. Before getting into the car, he leaned against it and took a long look around. Even from this distance she could see that his expression was one of disappointment. Finally, with a barely perceptible shake of his head, he slid into the driver's seat.

Apparently he'd finally decided there was no point in hanging around here, and was going off in search of greener pastures. Of course, a little nudge from Jake and Curly had probably helped him make up his mind.

Good-bye and good riddance, she thought as she watched him drive away. She resisted the temptation to stick her head out the window and shout, ''And don't come back!'' She started to turn away when she caught sight of Jake and Curly, also watching Stanly's departure.

Jake glanced up toward her window. When she raised her hands over her head and clasped them together in a gesture of victory, a broad grin came over his features.

One of her problems, at least, was solved. There was still that other matter to be dealt with, though—how to make Reese understand that she was serious about leaving. She pushed the painful thought from her mind. She'd worry about that when the time came.

If things went smoothly, and there were no more unforeseen occurrences, she could say her good-byes to Mattie and the kids, and then be on her way by tomorrow morning.

Chapter Seventeen

The first thing Reese noticed when he pulled into the driveway was that Stanly's rental car was nowhere in sight. What was going on around here? he wondered, as Jake and Curly came ambling up. Everything about the two ranch hands told him something was in the air.

"What are you two grinning about?" he asked, getting out of the Jeep. "You look like a couple of Cheshire cats. And where's Stanly?"

Curly shifted his weight from one leg to the other, while Jake developed a sudden interest in examining cloud formations overhead.

Curly was the first to speak. "Well, boss, he's on his way to the airport. Seems he decided to cut his visit short."

"Why would he do that?" Not that Reese had any objections to being rid of their obnoxious guest, but he had the feeling there was more to it than that.

"I can't imagine," Jake replied, his expression as guileless as that of a newborn baby. "We did everything we could to make him feel welcome. We even let him ride ol' Pete, when he insisted he wanted to."

"Ride Pete? Why would he . . ." Reese's voice trailed off as he thought about this. "Rode Pete, did he? Not for long, I'll bet."

" 'Bout five minutes, tops,'' Curly drawled.

"That right?'' Although Reese's tone was serious, there was a hint of laughter in his eyes.

"He, ah, had a few last words before he left.'' This was from Jake. "He said Pete should be taken out and shot. Oh—and that you oughta fire the lot of us.''

"Hmmm.'' Although Reese rubbed his chin thoughtfully as if considering this, there was a twinkle of amusement in his eyes.

He was still chuckling as he entered the house. He felt as if a huge weight had been lifted from his shoulders. Now that Stanly was out of the way he could concentrate on more important matters, such as telling Amy he loved her.

He almost collided with her as she came out of the utility room just off the kitchen, her arms full of laundry still warm from the clothes drier.

Surprised, she took a step backward to maintain her balance. Instinctively, he reached out to steady her, then stopped himself. He was aware of how her nearness could make him lose all sense of reason. If he expected to present his case clearly and rationally, he needed to be in complete control of his faculties. *Don't blow this,* he told himself, as he drew a deep, calming breath.

He had no idea how to work up to telling her he loved her and didn't want her to go away. He couldn't just blurt it out. "I hear Stanly decided to cut his visit short,'' he said, because it was the only thing he could think of to say.

A little smile played around the corners of her mouth. "I think Jake and Curly had a hand in helping him make the decision to leave. I doubt if he'll be back. I'm pretty sure we managed to convince him there's no reason for him to hang around.''

There was an uncomfortable silence, as if they were both reflecting on the ramifications of Stanly's departure.

Amy was the first to speak. "Now that he's out of the way, there's no reason for me to stay any longer," she said briskly. "I'll be leaving in a day or two. You'll have to excuse me now. I have a million things to do to get ready to go." She started to brush past him.

Reese felt a stab of panic. If he didn't do something soon, she was going to walk right out of his life—while he stood there tongue-tied, unable to tell her how much he loved her. It was now or never.

"Amy, wait."

She looked back at him curiously. "Yes?"

But before he could say more, the back door opened and Kevin came running in, calling, "Hey, Chrissie . . ." His words trailed off as he glanced around the room. "Is Chrissie in here?"

"I thought she was playing with you out in the barn," Amy said.

"She was. We were playing hide-and-seek, but when it was her turn to hide, I couldn't find her. I thought maybe she came in the house."

Take it easy, Reese told himself, fighting back a pang of uneasiness. Just because Kevin couldn't find her, that didn't necessarily mean she was missing. There were any number of places she might be. "Where have you looked for her?" he asked.

Kevin's forehead furrowed in concentration. "All over the barn, and the tack shed, and in the front yard."

Mattie came into the room just in time to hear this last exchange. "Chrissie's missing?" A shadow of alarm crossed her face. "How could she be? I just checked on her and Kevin a few minutes ago."

"Now, Mattie, we don't know for sure that she's actually missing," Reese said reassuringly, as much to ease his own fears as Mattie's. "Let's look around inside the house first.

Maybe she's up in her room.'' But when a quick but thorough check of the house turned up no sign of the little girl, he began to feel a little prickle of fear.

In a short time every available person on the ranch was pressed into service searching all the areas near the house and barn. When the results proved fruitless, they gathered in front of the barn to discuss what to do next.

''It's pretty clear she's not anyplace close by, boss.'' Will Adler pushed his hat back on his head. ''I think it's time to launch a major search effort.''

At the foreman's words, a heavy weight settled in Reese's midsection. Until now he'd been able to tell himself Chrissie wasn't really missing, that she was playing her own form of hide-and-seek. Or that she'd fallen asleep—maybe in some shadowy corner of the barn, where nobody had noticed her. It would be easy to miss seeing such a small child.

But they couldn't take the chance that that was the case. If she had wandered off, every second they hesitated lessened the possibility that she would be found safely.

''I'll start calling people,'' Mattie said.

Reese nodded. There was no time to waste.

Once Mattie made a few strategic phone calls, it didn't take long for word to spread that help was needed out at the Cavanaugh place. Neighbors and friends began arriving, some on horseback, others in Jeeps or other four-wheel-drive vehicles. They brought large, heavy-duty flashlights, lengths of rope, anything that might be useful in a rescue attempt. ''Don't worry, we'll find her,'' they said reassuringly.

The search effort was under way in a very short time. While the searchers with vehicles began combing the maze of back roads and trails that crisscrossed the ranch, those on horseback fanned out in all directions. They moved slowly away from the area around the house and barn, scanning every depression on the rough ground, every rock formation or irregularity where a small child might take shelter.

Reese noticed that the sky had darkened, and a chilly wind was blowing up. It looked as if they might be in for some rain. A stab of panic ran through him at the thought of Chrissie—so tiny and helpless—being out in it. Rainstorms around here could be pretty violent. Gullies and ditches filled up quickly, and water picked up force as it gushed down hillsides.

Even if the rain didn't materialize, she would be chilled to the bone in no time. It had been warm this morning when Mattie had gotten her into her play clothes. She wasn't dressed for this kind of weather.

A tightness rose in his chest as he recalled how cute she'd looked in her red T-shirt and jeans, her ponytail tied back with a red ribbon.

How could he have allowed this to happen? he berated himself. He should have . . . well, he wasn't sure what, but he should have done *something*. He was Chrissie's guardian, and it was up to him to protect her, to keep her safe.

He'd never forgive himself if she wasn't found safely. Both of the children were so much a part of him now that he couldn't imagine not having them. He knew the rest of his life would be empty beyond belief if he ever had to give either of them up for any reason.

Yet he'd had no qualms about asking Amy to give them up, a little voice reminded him.

It wasn't the same thing, he thought defensively. When he'd asked Amy to relinquish any claim on them, it was because he knew that was what was best for them.

But did that make it any easier on her? that same voice nagged.

The thought of turning the kids over to him must have torn her heart out. Yet she'd agreed to do it because—as he'd pointed out—it was better for the kids. He winced at the thought of how insufferably arrogant he must have sounded.

And what had he offered her in return? A quick divorce or annulment, once his purpose had been accomplished. Oh, he'd said she'd be welcome to come and visit as often as she liked, as if he were bestowing some great favor on her. Of course, he'd still be the one who had custody of the kids.

Instead of throwing his weight around, and reminding her of all the advantages he could give them that she couldn't, why hadn't he been looking for some kind of solution that wouldn't have been so painful for her?

He could hardly believe he'd been so unfeeling. True, he'd been convinced he was doing the right thing for Kevin and Chrissie—and for *himself,* his conscience reminded him. But what about Amy? Had he ever once stopped to consider what he was doing to *her?*

Once Chrissie was found safely, and she *would* be—he wouldn't let himself think otherwise—he'd settle things with Amy. He had so much to apologize to her for, so many reasons to beg her forgiveness. . . .

His attention was brought back to the matter at hand as a few cold, wet raindrops worked their way under his collar and rolled down his neck. He felt a sense of urgency as the rain began to come down in earnest. He shivered, not for himself but at the thought of the little girl huddled up somewhere out there, maybe taking shelter under a bush or a shrub, cold and frightened.

He fought the urge to spur his horse into a run, reminding himself that he could do more harm than good if he went rushing off headlong. He could easily ride right past her without even seeing her.

Forcing a patience he didn't feel, he reined the horse to a stop and took a long look around. The slope was becoming steeper now, and up above, the sparse brush was starting to give way to thick trees. He watched the other searchers slowly make their way up the hill.

He caught a glimpse of Amy about twenty or thirty yards to his right. Although the wide brim of her hat hid her features, her attention to the task at hand was evident in her every movement. She moved her horse forward a few steps at a time, stopping to look carefully to each side.

He started to urge his horse on, when something about the tilt of Amy's head caught his attention. She was leaning forward in the saddle just slightly, as if examining something. Reaching down, she picked an object off a clump of brush.

Hope leaped in him. What had she found?

As if she sensed his gaze on her, she glanced in his direction. When she saw that he was looking at her, she held her hand up. Although he couldn't tell what she was holding from this distance, her excitement communicated itself to him.

He cut across the slope and reined his horse to a stop next to hers. "What did you find?" he asked, keeping his voice low. He didn't want to arouse any false hopes in the other searchers.

She showed him the scrap of muddy, tattered ribbon, barely recognizable as being red. Once again, a quick image crossed his mind, of a ponytail tied with a red ribbon. His heart slammed against his chest. There was no need for words as his gaze met Amy's. Together, they urged their horses up the slope.

They might have missed the small figure if it hadn't been

for the red shirt. Chrissie was curled up in a little ball beneath the overhang of a rock, drawing on the scant protection it offered from the elements. At the sound of approaching hoofbeats she sat up, rubbing her eyes with tiny fists. Her face was dirty and tear-streaked.

Amy reached her a few seconds before Reese. Slipping from the saddle, she dropped to her knees and drew the shivering child into her arms.

Reese felt almost weak with relief. Dismounting, he blinked rapidly, and drew several deep breaths to ease the tightness in his throat. Excited shouts of, ''They've found her!'' echoed across the hillside as the news was relayed to the other searchers.

He knelt on one knee, but when he reached out to take the little girl, she shook her head and buried her face against Amy.

He backed off, reminding himself that Amy had been an important figure in her life long before he'd come into the picture. He took his jacket off and wrapped it around both of them.

''Why did you run off?'' Amy asked gently. ''We were all very worried about you.''

''That man—he kept saying he wanted me and Kevin to come and live with him.''

''You mean Stanly?'' Amy brushed the hair away from Chrissie's forehead.

She nodded emphatically. ''I came up here to hide from him, and then I got lost and couldn't find my way back, and it started to rain and I got cold. . . . I don't have to go with him, do I?''

Reese cleared his throat so he could speak around the lump that had formed there. ''No, sweetheart. We won't ever let anyone take you away.''

She twisted around in Amy's arms to look at him. ''And you and Aunt Amy will always live here with me?''

He found himself at a loss for words. He could he make that promise? Maybe it was too late to talk Amy into staying. He felt a stab of guilt. If she went away he had nobody but himself to blame. If only he'd told her sooner how he felt. If only he'd *realized* sooner that he loved her.

He was spared having to reply by the approach of the other searchers. Glancing over his shoulder, he realized they were surrounded by a circle of riders, all grinning broadly. He could have sworn there was a suspicious moistness in more than one pair of eyes.

Chrissie allowed herself to be taken from Amy's arms long enough for Amy to mount her horse. Then the child was passed back to her. It was a triumphant procession that accompanied her down the hill. Reese rode by her side solicitously, ready to steady her and her precious charge if her horse should happen to stumble.

After a quick examination by the local doctor, Chrissie was pronounced in good condition, despite a few scratches, and turned over to Mattie's capable care for a hot bath, some nourishing soup, and a healthy dose of TLC.

Once the searchers had been thanked and the last of them had ridden off, Amy led Smoky into a stall in the now-deserted barn and started to unsaddle her. All at once she felt unbelievably weary. The stresses and tensions of the past few days had robbed her of her last remaining reserves of strength.

Now that Chrissie was safe and Stanly was out of the picture, she knew it was time to get on with her plans to leave here.

But Chrissie's words to Reese came back to her: ''You and Aunt Amy will always live here with me?''

True, she hadn't promised she would stay. Still, there was no telling what it might do to the child if she were to leave suddenly. She wondered if it might be better to postpone her departure for a while, until Chrissie was feeling safe and secure again. If she stayed much longer, though, there was the chance she might inadvertently give away her feelings for Reese. Not for anything in the world would she have him know she had broken the terms of their agreement by falling in love with him.

She'd make up her mind what to do about this dilemma later. Right now she couldn't even summon the strength to make a simple decision. She felt completely drained, both physically and emotionally.

Once she had the saddle and blanket off Smoky, she reached for a brush and began grooming the little mare with long, smooth strokes. She found the repetitive motion soothing to her tired nerves. Here in the semidarkness of the barn, the only sounds were Smoky's even breathing and the rustle of straw as the animals moved around in their stalls.

"Amy, are you in here?"

Her hand paused in midstroke. She didn't feel up to talking to Reese right now. Maybe if she just didn't move or say anything he'd leave.

But Smoky gave her away by glancing back at her and nickering softly, as if asking why she had stopped brushing her. She could hear Reese's booted footsteps as he walked across the cement floor of the barn. He covered the distance to the stall in a few long strides. "There you are," he said. "I wondered where you'd gone off to."

"I, ah, thought I'd let Mattie have Chrissie to herself for a little while. She blames herself that Chrissie ran off and got lost. She feels she should have been watching closer."

"If anyone is to blame, it's Bender, for scaring the poor

little kid half to death,'' Reese said, coming into the stall. ''But I didn't come looking for you so we could talk about Bender. We have other matters to discuss.''

''Wh-what other matters?'' There was something in his manner—an air of determination—that she found somewhat overpowering.

''For starters, about your going away.''

She drew a deep sigh. Why couldn't he let it drop? ''We've been through this. We had an agreement.''

''It wasn't carved in stone, for Pete's sake.'' A nervous whinny from Smoky reminded him his voice was rising. ''Amy, you can't leave,'' he said, his tone calmer and less intense.

She was getting tired of this sparring. ''Why not?''

''Well, ah, the kids still need you. You heard what Chrissie said when we found her up on the hill.''

''The kids will get along just fine. They have you and Mattie. They don't need me.'' She was relieved that she could say the words so calmly. Her voice didn't even break.

Several heartbeats of time stretched into what seemed an eternity before Reese asked, ''What if *I* need you?''

The question, barely audible, caught her off guard. What did he need her for? To keep Kevin and Chrissie happy and secure here? As a buffer between him and Francine— or any other woman who might be a threat to his precious freedom?

And was she willing to accept being needed as a substitute for being loved?

As these questions whirled through her mind, Reese took a step toward her. Instinctively, she backed away, aware of how easily she could lose her ability to make a rational decision if he stood too close to her. When she came up against the rough wood of the wall behind her, it occurred to her just how small this enclosure was, with two people and a horse in it. There was hardly room to keep any kind of distance between her and Reese. In the stillness, she was sure he must be able to hear the thudding of her heart.

Almost in a whisper, she asked, "What exactly do you mean, you need me?"

He didn't reply for so long that she began to wonder if he intended to at all. Finally, when the silence between them was almost a tangible thing, he said, "I mean the rest of my life won't be worth two cents if you're not here to share it with me. I love you."

Amy stared at him, too overcome with emotion to formulate any coherent response. *Do something, say something,* a little voice in her head shouted. Reese had just told her he loved her, and all she could do was stand there like a ninny, unable to say a word.

Reese apparently misinterpreted her silence. "I know I'm not much for pretty speeches, but you have to believe me—I *do* love you," he said, his voice low and husky with feeling. "I guess I didn't realize it until you started making plans to leave. Please stay. If you go away you'll not only be hurting the kids, but you'll be hurting yourself and me. We belong together."

As Amy tried to pull her scattered thoughts together, Reese took the brush from her and put it on the shelf, then took her in his arms. In spite of her weariness, all her senses leaped to sudden, vibrant life at his touch.

"I know we agreed that our marriage would be just a business arrangement," he said, "but that was before I fell in love with you. Do you think you could learn to love me in return—just a little bit, at least? I'm willing to wait as long as it takes. . . ."

All at once a little bubble of happiness welled up inside her, until she was so full of joy she felt her heart would burst. She finally found her voice. ''Oh, Reese, I don't have to learn to love you. I already love you.''

At first, Reese looked as if he hardly dared believe what he was hearing. Then the questioning expression in his eyes was replaced by something else—something that sent a little thrill of excitement through Amy.

''Did the boss say whether he wants us to start bringing that herd down from the summer pasture, or wait until we get the hay crop in?'' Curly asked as he and Will strolled into the barn.

''I haven't had a chance to talk to him about it,'' the foreman replied. ''Where is he, anyhow? I haven't seen him since he came back with the searchers. . . .''

His words trailed off as he spotted the two figures in one of the stalls, almost hidden by the little mare. Reese's arms were around Amy, and she was standing on tiptoe to meet his kiss.

Putting a finger to his lips, Will motioned Curly out of the barn. When they were out of earshot, he said, ''I don't think I'll bother him with minor matters just now. It looks like the boss and his lady are kinda busy at the moment.''

Withdrawn From Montgomery-Floyd Regional Library